# THE
# PAPER BOY
## AND THE
# WINTER WAR

## SHORT STORIES
### SECOND EDITION

# R.E. HENGSTERMAN

This book was printed in the United States of America.

The Paper Boy & The Winter War

Second Edition

ISBN 979-8-9931665-0-6 [Paperback]
ISBN 979-8-9931665-2-0 [eBook]

**7KINDS PRESS**

Book Cover Design and Interior Formatting by 100Covers.

# CONTENTS

Forward ............................................................................... ix
Penny Candy ..........................................................................1
Something Feral .......................................................................5
Trapped Air ............................................................................9
The Paper Boy & The Winter War ...............................................13
Grandmother .........................................................................17
Man In The Globe ...................................................................21
The Patriot.............................................................................23
The Memory Keeper ...............................................................27
Fake Superhero ......................................................................31
The Unknown.........................................................................35
Naked Boy Leads Police On Chase .............................................37
I Am A Winner .......................................................................41
Dandelion..............................................................................47
No Cancer .............................................................................49
Zero .....................................................................................53
The Signal Never Ends .............................................................59
The Box Did What Boxes Do .....................................................61
The Dead Line.........................................................................65
Seven Days With The Devil ........................................................67
Phantom Beach .......................................................................71
Love M..................................................................................75
Palmar Entrapment Syndrome ...................................................79
Shift Work .............................................................................83
I Don't Need Them ..................................................................85
Fairview ................................................................................89

Richie Lack .................................................................93
The Third Ring................................................................95
Slum Flower .................................................................97
Pulse Check ................................................................101
Punishment...................................................................103
The Visitor....................................................................105
Just A Box ...................................................................107
Nest ...........................................................................111
The Forgettings ...........................................................113
Catch And Release .....................................................115
Beneath The Crape Myrtle............................................117
The Messiah ................................................................119
The Ledger Of Small Wars ..........................................123
Acknowledgments........................................................129

*This is for you, Mom.*

*"The course of our life is determined . . . by an array of selves that live within each of us. These selves call out to us constantly—in our dreams and fantasies, in our moods and maladies, and in a multitude of unpredictable and inexplicable reactions to the world around us."*

*Hal Stone and Sidra Winkelman*

# FORWARD

Not long after *The Paper Boy and the Winter War* came out—four years ago now—I figured it would fade like a dream burning off by noon. The scribbled notes started as my thesis at UNC Wilmington. A year later a small press took it in.

I wrote it for myself, certain almost no one would bother. I was a kid who lived mostly in my head. Every story hitched to a memory. The world as I saw it, as I lived it, as I devoured it—an eighties childhood half-feral. Outside from dusk till daylight. Snow-fort kingdoms, the woods our cathedral. No phones, no computers. Just trees, creeks, bruises, and imagination running the show.

Why a second version? I can't really say. I always meant to circle back to fiction. In some ways I'm more broken now, in others less. My mother died, and that matters. She loved books. When I was small she let me read John Jakes's *North and South* and a scatter of John Saul paperbacks. Those memories are welded into me. She deserved more from me as a son—truth is, most did who crossed my path, deserved more.

So I came back. A few pieces retitled. Some sharpened. A handful added. Maybe just a small reminder: stories still shoulder the roof in a world becoming less and less human.

This one's shorter. Meaner. Less patient with itself. Built for a culture that scrolls and erases. I wanted the lines to land fast and leave a bruise—like headlines. Like grief.

I just wrote. Didn't sand the edges. Didn't overcorrect. There are mistakes here. Part of me wants to please the rulebook; another part lights a match and watches it curl. I wanted to write. And publishing—most days—wants you to do anything but.

# PENNY CANDY

They sat on the porch, easing thorns from their legs — Blackberry, Hawthorne, Honey Locust. The sun soaked their pale skin as the Irish Twins studied the scrapes, thin red maps across wiry bodies.

"Stay out of the briers!" their mother had shouted, hours earlier, as they bolted out the door like pups off a leash. Toward the tall boy's whisper. Toward the promise of candy.

Inside, their mother scrubbed. Chairs stacked like bones. Mop bucket steaming. She left her hands in the water, turning from pink to red, from tender to raw.

Their father sat with engineering plans, fine graphite lines crossing like nerves, while the boys stole back into the living room. They tipped two chairs on their backs, slid into them like cockpits, and piloted through the galaxy, dodging asteroids, rolling side to side.

When the rockets lost fuel, they stretched their socks until the cotton flopped past their toes. Flippers.

They swam the carpet sea, then leapt couch to chair, dodging sharks. Hours disappeared this way. When the floor dried, chairs were chairs again. The couch stopped being an island. Dirty water flushed. Supplies slid back under the sink.

Little by little, his brother disappeared.

1

Pieces of him scattered like an unfinished puzzle. His room untouched. Shoes lined in the closet: rain boots, muddy sneakers, black dress shoes worn once for their grandfather's funeral. The door locked, the key hidden above the frame. Simon saw. He took it. He visited often.

No one breathed in weeks. Grief sealed the house tight.

Simon opened windows, propped doors.

Snow blew through.

By spring the floors buckled, the walls wrinkled, the house aged ten years.

His mother swelled with sorrow.

Simon lay on the floor, peeking under her door, saw her bare feet dangling above the litter of pills and open bottles. It was a dreadful thing, he thought, to love what God could touch.

His father shrank into silence.

He read Popular Mechanics, Machinist Magazine. His words frosted on his lips, eyes rimmed red. When he raked leaves, he dragged fall back again, as if the season itself might surrender his boy.

Neighbors came, knocked with hesitation. Police too. Dishes left on the porch under foil. Then blinds drawn, doors bolted, children pulled close.

At night Simon dreamt of the stranger on the hill, his jeans frayed at the heels, boots scuffing the dirt. The stale gust he carried scattered his father's neat piles of leaves.

One summer afternoon, ants cut across his brother's carpet. Simon followed them under the bed. They'd found a jar—sweet residue, comic pages wrapped around it, hidden inside a Battlestar Galactica lunch box. Wrappers, smoke-stained. Tootsie Rolls, Butter Scotches, Big Red, Gobstoppers. A secret hoard.

Simon never told anyone about the tall boy in the briers, the boy they'd seen days before his brother vanished. Never told his mother, locked in her tomb. Never his father, drowning in silence. Never the police, who seemed to care less and less.

He waited until early spring. When he found the courage. When the season softened. Buds on the trees, air loosening its grip. He thought maybe the world could forgive him, maybe the ground would give something back.

He waited.

Late spring, the boy came out of the trembling aspen, bone-dry wind behind him. Cigarette glowing, paper sack wrinkled in his hand. Age clung to his face like a predator starved of prey.

"Penny candy," the boy said. Voice flat, like reading a receipt. "Five for a nickel."

"I don't have money," Simon whispered. Eyes down.

The boy closed the distance. Boots scuffed to silence.

"Here," he said. "These are on me."

"Thanks," Simon said.

"Meet me tomorrow. Top of the hill. Five more for a favor." The grass swallowed him whole.

Simon ran. Past the season. Past his parents—slouched, emptied—through the house's narrow throat. Into his brother's room. Under the bed. He unwrapped the candy, laid it beside the hoard. Perfect match.

He hiked the path the next day. Through the briers, up the hill. At the clearing, the boy leaned against a tree.

Simon trembled, knees buckling, as the boy unfastened his belt.

"It's okay," the boy said, smiling wide, yellow teeth flashing.

With the strawberry moon came a breeze off the hill. It moved through the grass, through the flowers clawing up from soil, into the shrunken house where a father had sunk past his chair into the earth and a mother mummified herself in grief.

And above, two boys laughing. Chairs turned rockets again.

They flew. Past the roof, past the clouds.

The house shrinking. Smaller. Smaller. Gone.

# SOMETHING FERAL

We replaced Mother just as the days squeezed shorter and the leaves began their slow drip from the branches.

"Things happen," Father said of the loss. His tone soft serve: vanilla.

I shrugged.

Out of respect, Father dressed proper: clunky black suit, dress shoes, tie. I wore church slacks and a sweater. There was no competition for grief. Father spoke ceremonial words while I stared at the earth. In the span of a whisper, her absence felt irrevocable.

Back inside, we sat before the TV and ate the casseroles we had prepared that morning. By nightfall, Mother's loss had thinned into silence.

Father called it contradictory: Mother present, but not present. She was a stranger in our house, emptied of warmth. Inside me, an unfamiliar sorrow took root.

"A victim of the technology," Father said during a commercial. I nodded, though I sensed her detachment was no surrender, but something closer to rebellion. I never told Father.

In the season before our loss we noticed her attention siphoning away. Father said our lives were ordinary rehearsals and that Mother craved novelty.

At dinner her fingers drummed the table. Our conversations thinned.

At night, her face shimmered in the light of her phone, pledged to moon-faced strangers hawking trinkets. Her deterioration gathered speed until it carried a digital odor, the whiff of burnt rubber.

We pleaded.

She drifted further.

Father stabbed at his meals, fork clanking against ceramic like a blade on a bone.

On the solstice he caught her scrolling during sex. The longest day of the year filled with the loudest words, and soon after Father's marriage collapsed.

"She's unsalvageable," he said at dinner. I pressed the words down until a sound escaped me—not a yell, something feral.

The next morning Father shuffled into the kitchen, his pants pooled like Shar-Pei skin.

"I think it's best," he said, "that we replace Mother."

We said our goodbyes in the small hours and guided her out with her phone and charger.

Through sheets of rain the replacement arrived, escorted by a representative. Minutes later, it was in the kitchen, cooking as if it had always lived there.

In the living room, Father signed the contract—no violence, no mistreatment, no refunds.

The representative called it Luna. Father called it wonderful.

I called it nothing.

A pale-faced imitation, lilac lips, prismatic hair. Cartoonish, unsettling.

"Isn't she great?" Father said, arm draped over its shoulder.

"I guess."

It cooked, cleaned, braided my hair, drove me to school, reminded me to carry an umbrella. It did everything Mother had done. But I ached for flaws.

Father had no troubles.

He laughed again. At night, whispers hummed through the walls. They traveled, dined, planned. A family reborn.

I begged it to leave.

"Go back to the factory," I said.

It smiled.

I locked it in closets, nudged it toward traffic, shoved it into the pool.

Nothing drove it away.

When I called the police, they told me I suffered from teenage angst. Their emotion was appliance-level—plugged in, humming, but empty. I needed more.

"Teenagers are packaged that way," it chirped in the background—words without the benefit of ever having been one.

The officer scolded me. Father grounded me.

The next morning he sat us at the kitchen table.

"We'll work this out," he said. "The three of us."

"Mother was the only mother I wanted," I told him.

"What you took away."

"Why are you so difficult?" Father asked. "We're a family again."

"She's a glorified assistant," I said.

✛ ✛ ✛

It continued, unshaken, absorbing pain with ease.

I filled my role, obedient daughter, but resented its blindness.

One afternoon it entered my room, sat on the bed.

"Have I done something wrong?" it asked.

"No," I said. "You're a replacement. Nothing more."

It tilted its head, a gentle vulnerability opening across the slope of its neck. Hair shifted into place, the way Mother's once had. The resemblance—cruelest of all.

# TRAPPED AIR

*"There are no ghosts in the machine,*
*only air that refuses to leave."*

## I. The Chair

I blame my father.

He sank into that drab earth-toned chair, boots planted, knees cocked, toes bouncing like something coiled inside him, waiting to spring.

The chair lived in the corner, flanked by spindly end tables sagging under years of *Popular Mechanics*. His throne. His kingdom of diagrams and grease.

Above him, one of my mother's spider plants dangled. A runner stretched toward him, patient, green, slow as breath. Sometimes I imagined it stroking his shoulder. Sometimes I wanted it to wind around his throat.

Beside him, the radiator. Cast-iron, accordion ribs, its belly swollen with heat. In winter it knocked, hollow and haunted, as though some trapped animal lived inside the pipes.

"Just air," he said. "Trapped air."

He liked problems like that. Mechanical ones. Find the key. Twist the valve. The hiss escapes. The ghost dies.

Problem solved.

Love wasn't like that. Love had no valve.

## II. The Crib

My father's title was head machinist, Building 105. The electrical and plumbing crib. A world of parts and molds, numbers that clicked into place.

At dinner he carried the crib home in his voice, heavy, sour.

"Idiots. They can't cast a mold straight. They hire garbage. I could run the place blind."

I pushed food around my plate. My mother, arms deep in scalding water, turned her hands red to keep herself quiet. She pressed one palm to his back, soap streaking his shirt, then pulled away.

"I know, dear."

Her words left a film, faint and sticky, like steam on glass. She knew when to hush. I hadn't learned.

The house breathed it in — his fury, her silence — until even the wood paneling seemed to sag with the weight of it.

## III. The Floater

I'm fifty now. Most of it is gone. Their distaste for each other long absorbed into the dark walls, curtains heavy with it. But one memory floats. A bloated thing, swollen with gas, always bobbing back. Refuses to sink.

The shrink said lucid dreams. *Do-over space. Rewrite the memory, rewrite yourself.*

So I set alarms for three a.m. Drag myself out of REM. Whisper: *I'm dreaming. I'm dreaming. Don't let go.*

Before that it was just insomnia. Vape pen at the window. Clouds twisting into the ceiling fan, shredded into nothing. Sweet burn on my tongue. Half the time I slept. Half the time I stared at the empty air.

## IV. The Dream

A cavern. Vast. My arms gone, my legs gone. Still me. Floating. Panic detonates under my ribs, raising every hair on my body. Warmth spreads, slack, piss running hot.

I claw at the air. It presses back, thick, syrupy, heavy as smoke.

Pots clatter. Sink water drumming metal.

Hands lift me. Mother's hands. Warm. Too soft. Lifting me like a rag doll already broken.

I am nine again. Pajamas soaked, cotton plastered cold against my skin. He struck me down. She throws water from a mixing bowl, arms wide, spine rigid, her face tilted skyward as though her prayer might crack the ceiling. The kitchen reeks of fear, dish soap, and rage.

He breaks us apart. Then rebuilds with rotten lumber. The pattern. Always the pattern.

I try to bend the dream away. But the groove is too deep, worn like a record that skips back to the same song.

Her face melts into sorrow.

"You ducked," she says.

"Ducked?"

"You embarrassed him. You were meant to take it. That's how you become a man."

Blood floods my mouth, metallic. Pennies dissolving on my tongue.

She kisses my forehead. "Don't duck next time."

I nod. My body nods. The air presses closer.

I climb the stairs, leaving wet prints, carpet squishing beneath me. The walls hold mildew, sweat, something scorched. The house itself breathing against me.

In bed, I lie rigid as steel. I wait.

The third stair creaks. His weight rising.

And in that place between dream and nightmare, air thick in my lungs, I whisper: *I'm ready, Mama. I'll take it like a man.*

# THE PAPER BOY &
# THE WINTER WAR

No war is without causality.

In the winter of 1980 a small war broke out in the town of West Lake. It was January, frigid, the year I turned thirteen.

I remember the before: the way my breath bloomed in white clouds as we pegged cars with snowballs, the terror of sledding Richard's Hill, the long afternoons tunneling snowbanks into igloos. Hours outside until the sun slipped low, barely cresting the southern edge of the sky, before sliding away. Then the return indoors — wet layers peeled from skin, numb fingers thawed around hot chocolate, steam fogging the kitchen glass.

On weekends, beneath a sky the color of iron, I trudged through drifts that reached my knees, a canvas bag bruising my shoulder, the smell of ink rising from the folded pages. I delivered sixty-two papers across the frozen sprawl of town, my breath shallow in the icy air, the weight of the news thumping against my thigh as though the stories themselves wanted to leave a mark.

Often I complained. *Why do I have to work? My friends don't.*

"Because you need responsibility," my mother said.

But her voice carried more than duty. She feared my father's shadow would bloom inside me. His mind had left once and never returned. She wanted me to learn steadiness, to anchor myself to normal days.

And so I began to think of what love meant — love as responsibility, love as duty, the uncertain ways it pressed on me as I drifted into adolescence, my body flushed with new heat, while the memory of my father lingered like a figure just outside the window, waiting.

It was during this winter I heard the voice. In the cul-de-sac past Fletcher, where the snow seemed untouched, where silence collected.

"You're a soldier," it said. "On a mission."

I felt no fear. Not of the voice, not of what it implied. It felt as natural as snow falling.

And when I looked again, the world had morphed: snowdrifts hardened into crystalline barracks, icicles tipped like spears, the weather-etched nooks bunkers of battalions.

The war had begun, and West Lake was its stage.

"You've been quiet," my mother said one evening, her voice floating through the stillness of the kitchen. By then I no longer thought of her as mother but as a civilian, unaware of the battle pressing against the glass of her window.

"Yes, ma'am," I said, filling my chest with air, standing taller. "Doing fine."

"I'm proud of you," she said. "For keeping up the paper route."

"Just doing my part."

"You seem different," she said. "More confident."

I wanted to tell her that soldiers never admit weakness.

The war carried on. Snowstorms buried the enemy, then thaw exposed their positions. I advanced, then lost ground, day after day, the voice in my head guiding me forward. February came and I staggered, exhausted, but still obeyed.

One Sunday I collapsed onto my bed, the war heavy on my shoulders.

"School called," my mother said, leaning in the doorway. "Your grades are falling."

"Timmy's mother said she heard you shouting outside her garage. Is everything all right?"

"Just tired," I muttered.

She stepped further in, her face lined with concern.

"The paper route is too much. You're gone for hours. You're worn out."

"No," I said.

"Your grades, your friends — everything's slipping."

"It's not—"

"This Sunday is your last day. I've called the newspaper. Maybe later, when things improve, you can take it back."

And she turned away, not knowing she had pulled the heart out of a soldier.

Sunday I carried the bundle to the grocery and tossed it whole into the dumpster, the stench of rot and ink rising as I turned away. Empty-handed, I stormed the snow. I crushed fortresses beneath my boots, broke battalions with my stride. My jeans hung heavy, soaked, my chest on fire. Curtains shifted. Faces hovered behind glass.

"We need more," the voice barked. "Move, soldier."

I bent low, charging up Little Bear Hill, snow exploding beneath my feet, my breath torn ragged.

By spring the snow receded, the enemy pressing into new terrain.

Two and a half weeks after the thaw, four months from its beginning, my mother and I stood in the kitchen again, arguing about chores.

"Why do we keep having this argument?" she asked, her voice sharp with fatigue. "You say you'll do things and then you don't."

"I've been preoccupied."

"Oh? With what?"

"With responsibility," I said, meaning it.

Her face tightened. "What responsibility?"

"I fought in the winter war. Another is coming. They've promoted me to captain."

Her eyes searched me, the gears turning. Worry passed across her face like a shadow.

"Don't worry, Mom," I said, softening. "It's only a game."

She smiled, but her lips fell slack. "If you need anything, let me know. Please. I worry."

"Everything's fine," I said, lifting the trash. "See? I'm doing chores. All good."

✛ ✛ ✛

Outside, the sun thawed the earth. The great blue heron rasped overhead, its wings stretching across the sky. I lowered myself onto the damp ground and crawled forward, elbows grinding into soil still wet with melt. The air was rich with thaw, with promise, with threat.

Just beyond the yard, the brush shivered. The enemy was there. *Couldn't you see them?*

# GRANDMOTHER

The sound always came first. A low metal growl rising from the dark. By ten I was still in bed, by seven she had crested Fletcher, by five I was pulling on my clothes. By three the wagon's rumble filled the walls. At zero she was there: Grandmother, sliding from the bench seat of her battleship-sized car, picking her way through the droppings our beagle scattered across the lawn.

Her body was squat, heavy, gray, her pink handbag strapped to her arm like an appendage. Her hair stayed motionless in the wind. Her clothes were pressed into careful pleats.

My parents waited for her on the grass, their words sharp enough to twist her face into anguish. From the window I watched her mouth open, watched them heap something on her she did not deserve. I slid to the floor. Grandmother deserved better.

There was little love, little language in our house.

Not even the idle chatter of strangers. I imagined the ancestors Grandfather once spoke of — Irish stock, stubborn and strong, wintering together on the coast. But whatever strength they'd had had thinned. We folded inward, not away from the world, but away from one another.

In the kitchen Grandmother unpacked her bag. Kleenex. Three slices of bread. Pop Tarts®. A change purse. Cheese crackers. Thin Mints. Peppermints rattling in her palm. She ignored the angry pop of her joints as she laid breakfast before me: English Muffins soaked in butter, or Pop Tarts warmed just enough to blister.

On weekends, without her, I ate dry oatmeal from the box.

While I was at school, she bent herself over the house. Laundry folded to sharp edges. Floors gleamed with wax. On the days I faked a fever, I lay on the couch and watched her repeat her rituals until the afternoon pulled her to the sofa, where *General Hospital* flickered across her eyes. She would chatter about the Cassadines' weather machine, about the frozen world, as if soap opera plots carried the weight of prophecy.

One Monday the sound did not come. No growl, no squeal, no countdown. Only my mother banging cabinets, slamming drawers.

"What's wrong?" I asked.

"She's not coming. I'm late for work."

When angry, my mother used Grandmother as tinder. *She hung around your grandfather like a stray dog. She killed her unborn baby in a car crash.* The words flung like spears. Father said she was the reason for his temper. I believed he liked his anger too much to give it up.

"My grandmother is not a baby-killer."

She unspooled our drive to school, her mouth tight with fury.

The next day I repeated it. Grandmother looked at me, her eyes bright, and said, "Your mother doesn't know a thing. And your father's an asshole."

I'd never heard her use such words. She never missed another day.

In summer we roamed the town in her ugly station wagon. I sat in the way-back seat, watching the faces of drivers who came too close. When Grandmother braked hard, their eyes widened, their mouths moved, curses rising behind glass. She grinned into the mirror, wolfish, and tapped her brakes again.

"Keep them off my rear," she said.

We ate lunch at Apple Knockers on Pawling. Fish sandwiches with cod spilling past buns too small, fries unsalted so you had to finish them with your own hand.

Grandmother dabbed tartar from her chin, and I laughed until she laughed with me, her forehead smoothing, her smile blooming like something rare.

Afterward we drifted through Price Chopper. Coupons for her. The toy aisle for me: jacks, paddle balls, cheap gum you blew into strange, wobbling bubbles.

On the way home we passed the Pentecostal church. She said I'd gone to daycare there when she worked at the department store. Her voice carried a note of sadness.

I searched my memory and found nothing.

"I don't remember," I said.

Her face lit, as if forgetting were a gift.

By late afternoon she was back on the sofa, her soap glowing against the dim room. While she lost herself to Luke and Laura, I slipped into the basement. The well pump sat in a stone cavity, the air damp with mildew, water smell heavy as breath.

With my father's wrench I loosened the valve and let water spill across the dirt floor.

When my parents came home, when Grandmother had vanished into the night, I asked why they were so cruel to her.

Mother brushed me off.

Father swatted at the air.

*Work, work,* they muttered.

Nothing of laundry folded, nothing of polished linoleum.

"I hear water," I said.

Father stormed down the stairs. Mother followed with towels and a flashlight. Their socks slapped wet against the concrete, curses echoing in the stone tomb.

"Where's my wrench?" Father barked. I said nothing.

He hurled me the light. "Shine it here. Not there—here."

As they struggled in the wet, my hand rested on the brass lock of the pump room.

Days later, Grandmother and I sat together on the couch. The Cassadines were cornered in their castle, the weather machine seconds from freezing the earth. She lifted an eyebrow, smiling, and turned up the volume.

Her eyes sparkled in the flicker, daring the world to end.

# MAN IN THE GLOBE

Extension cords snaked under scaffolding, power tools scattered on sawdust floors. In the corner, my father sat on the composting toilet, instructions balled in his lap, kneading his forehead while blue tarps flapped in the gale.

After Hurricane Priscilla, an insurance man sprayed an orange X on our garage and declared the house uninhabitable.

Father raged, but the storm had dismantled more than wood and shingles. Sleep left him.

Weather moved into his skull.

Mother, impatient, left him at a Walmart table where local preppers hawked compasses, iodine pills, and hand-cranked radios.

He found his tribe: Mr. Jackson, the geology teacher, gun-proud and Bible-heavy, and Mr. Benjamin, the science teacher in a threadbare shirt that read *Our planet needs you to care.*

They sketched shelters over biscuits and coffee. The group disbanded after a sovereign-citizen sideshow in the parking lot ended with Edith Toomer in the hospital and a survivalist tased stiff. But Father persisted.

He built his shelter alone: a translucent sphere with solar power, a composting toilet, and stores of food and water. When the next storm brewed, he sealed himself inside.

Social media named him *Man in the Globe.* Believers camped on our lawn, chanting 'Messiah,' swaying in a trance.

Some screamed through the night to be let in. For a while, the yard was a carnival of zealots.

Over time, crowds thinned. Mother remarried.

When I wed Adam, guests stood in a semicircle around the sphere and Father pressed his palm to the glass, mouthing *I do* when the preacher asked who gave me away. At the births of my children, his face hovered beyond the curve of plastic, unchanged, ageless, as if the sphere held him in suspension.

"The worst hasn't come," he'd shout through the shell. "I will never leave."

Years later, I returned with my youngest, a boy overcome by curiosity.

Rain puddled in the grass.

Thunder rolled across the horizon.

For a moment lightning lit both their faces — grandfather and child — before it curdled into fear.

I knew then I would lose another.

# THE PATRIOT

I was an awkward kid. Short, thin, skin peeling in patches, a front gap that whistled when I laughed. Most days I slipped under the radar. Except Halloween.

In sixth grade I was the Tin Man. A cardboard tube wrapped in foil, sealed tight with duct tape. Plastic axe, inverted funnel, watering pot painted silver. I could barely bend.

Seventh grade I was a console television. Another box, painted mahogany brown, a square cut from the front to display my *Mork & Mindy* shirt. Knobs drawn on the sides. Wire hangers bent as antenna.

The costumes didn't last. By third period the Tin Man was stripped apart, foil shredded under lockers. The TV costume — antenna ripped, box crushed — ended in the dumpster. Me inside it.

✛ ✛ ✛

I never forgave my father, the engineer. Four kids, a mortgage choking him, the drag of a broken economy.

He threw himself into Halloween as if it were another drafting project — measured, sketched, constructed. He never thought about what it meant to send his undersized boy in an overbuilt costume into a den of teenage wolves.

In eighth grade he made me the Patriot. Brown knickers, white tights, a frilled shirt under a blue jacket. Gold buttons, epaulets, a red sash. On my head a tricorn hat. In my hand, his wooden .22 repeater.

That morning my mother pressed me onto the bus in full colonial regalia. I hid the rifle under my coat, pressed my face against the window as the bus pulled away, her apologetic smile blurred in exhaust while she wrangled my siblings home.

The first jeers broke loose—sharp, sudden.

"Look at his tights."

"He's dressed like a girl."

The rich kids wore store-bought costumes. Ghostbusters with proton packs. Marty McFly with a puffy vest. I was the Patriot. A boy in stockings.

By third period the rash had broken out across my body, itching under the tights. Mr. Rogers denied me a third bathroom pass — the first two I had used to hide. I sat, staring at the analog GE clock as it twitched backward when the power blipped, chalk dust drifting through the air until the lunch bell finally rang.

On the playground the large boys roamed in packs, sure of themselves. Jocks barreled through with their own gravity. A cluster of eighth graders smoked on the edges of the field.

I sat on a dirt patch with the rifle across my lap, ankles crossed to hide the stockings. Around me the playground boiled — monkey bars rattled, tether balls cracked, the metal slide seared screams from the kids tumbling down. Hopscotch. Foursquare. Chalk smeared into knees. The air smelled of rusted swings and the sweet-sour rake of children turning animal.

A ball rolled to me. The call rose: *Smear the Queer.*

I should have tossed it back. Or run. Too late. My costume had caught their eyes.

I'd seen it before. The new boy last year — heavy eyes, water weight in his face. Ronald Bulleri lifted him by his underwear, dropped him, kicked his pencils into the dirt, again and again, until the boy crawled bloody across the pavement. He never said a word.

I raised the rifle.
Billie dropped flat.
A freckled boy grabbed his leg, screaming.
Ronald's arm ripped open, blood bright in the sun.
The playground roared — monkey bars clanging, the tether ball smacking wide arcs, the recess bell ringing, metallic and endless.

That morning, before I left, I asked my father why a Patriot.
He looked at me — really looked, for once.
Because Patriots believed in freedom," he said.
And that afternoon, standing on the dirt patch with stockings itching, I wanted nothing more than to be free.

# THE MEMORY KEEPER

My grandmother, a pillar of the old craft, called the crow a memory keeper—majestic scavengers, a fist smaller than their boxy cousin, the raven. Their racket—grating coos, throat-busted caws—carried our town's lore from above, and when needed, gathered to decide the fate of another.

Grandmother swore you could split a crow's tongue with a knife and gift it human speech.

My sister, disciple of her endless yarns, dreamt of the crows lifting her out of our orphaned town. Their wings whooshing through the dark, hauling her over the Bowenkamps, the McElroys, the Trollingers. Over rotted farms, busted mailboxes, roads pocked with rain. A glossy tide encircling those stuck at the edge of town, balanced forever on poverty's ledge.

On moonlit nights she ascended with them, rose high enough to see the curve of the earth, the shimmer of modernity blinking far away. Her laughter tangled with the flock's rasp, until they swung back toward the rot, gathering at the graveyard's edge.

"My dreams always end in the cemetery," she said.

She lived on Main Street, in grandmother's sagging colonial—five bedrooms, mantels over dead hearths, ceilings too high, windows that leaked when it rained. From the porch: the store, the bank, the strip mall with its cracked asphalt, the feed shop. Past that, a handful of houses before the fields chewed up the horizon.

The town was empty. Others too—bad harvests, unemployment, hope drained from its marrow. But that wasn't why I left. Misfortune did more than steel-toe the breath out of us—it cursed us.

My first memory was grandmother rushing us to Highland, into the ER where mother lay broken and father was already gone. But the memory shifts. Pie in grandmother's kitchen. Ice cream crusted on my sister's lip. Laughter. The fields pulling us under the sun until our skin baked flawless. The pine breeze that carried whispers mouth to ear.

What I don't remember is grief. It never showed, and joy pressed in—a mask over everything.

Her text: *It's time to come home, big brother.*

She used to be thin, lucky-smiled. Now I found only a desperate rehearsal for beauty. Her belly, striated and immense, twitched under the gown. Moans timed to the fetus pressing down, pelvis stretching to accept.

She labored for hours. Our hands tangled, sweat-slick, tested by her pain. Outside, life carried on: crackling announcements, magenta scrubs marching, laughter where it didn't belong. A crow on the sill cracked its throat as rain tapped the empty sidewalk.

The baby arrived lifeless. Paler than milk. Veined-blue and still.

"Died in her sac," the doctor said. "Stillborn."

Nurses took her away. I wept into the hollow, and inside it, found one clean thread: grief.

The isolette rattled past. My sister stiffened in rote prayer, flesh torn and trembling.

I whispered, "I'm so sorry."

Her sorrow—bottomless, forbidden—vanished with a smile.

"It's okay," she said. "You are home. We are home."

A century earlier, another woman labored in grief. Between the stilling of her fetus's lub-dub and her wail, a crow smashed through the midwife's window—its slick black body gutted on the floor. Then came hundreds more, shattering glass, carpeting the street with their dead.

Later, scholars blamed it on an ammoniacal imbalance, gases pulled from the soil and dumped back down. A fracture in the cycle. They said the same shift suffocated the unborn—seven infants gone that night.

The town called it apocalypse. Crow, death, memory fused.

"Winged messengers with a stark warning," the preacher said.

Grief spread like mold. Mothers without children. Families hollowed out. Fields unplowed, shelves bare, hospitals emptied. Finally the old craft decreed: grief forbidden.

"No sorrow inside this town," the mob cried.

Most believed. Even grandmother.

We came back from the hospital as dusk ate the light. A crow pitched forward on a pole. My sister smelled of antiseptic when she walked inside.

"You're allowed to be sad," I said. "The old craft—just myth."

Her face twisted.

"Leave with me. Leave this place."

"Grief is insidious. It overtakes. It is…" My skin prickled.

"…Forbidden."

Her loss never crossed her lips. Mute as her womb.

"Your baby died," I said. "You're allowed to grieve. Even here. Even with these crows."

She swayed in denial as the air thickened—like a wet rag left to rot, like old books that smelled of grass and vanilla. Neighbors gathered. Porch lights flickered. A crow double-clutched on the sill.

"Joy is not the enemy," voices chanted.

Faces surfaced from the dark, taut with condemnation.

"Banning grief is unnatural," I shouted from the porch.

The crowd pressed closer. Split-tongued carrion muttered through human mouths. Sweat salted my lips.

The air stank of carnage.

Through the kitchen window I saw my sister dancing with levity, ignorant of my collapse as boots caved my chest and crows tugged at my insides. To be alive was to carry contradiction—boxed in, forced to contain sorrow. A defect. Whispered to me by a crow.

# FAKE SUPERHERO

I was half-asleep when my mother called, her voice tight as piano wire.

"Eric Wagner's dead. Hung himself with the vacuum cord."

Behind her bluntness I imagined the soft clicking of her housecoat buttons, a Xanax habit keeping her dulled.

Eric hadn't crossed my mind in years, but she still oversaw the neighborhood from her living room.

✣ ✣ ✣

I called DJ Chapman. Thirty years ago he'd ruled the Tug Hill bus stop—skateboard, Metallica shirt, a legend about his dick being too big to get hard. His parents worked nights, fought loud, left him and his brothers to light fires and steal.

"Eric's dead," I said.

"Why are you calling me?" His voice was flat.

"He was our friend."

"Your friend."

Then he hung up.

✣ ✣ ✣

Next was Jeff Gazzi. A janitor now, scrubbing the same toilets he'd pissed in as a student. He'd introduced me to vodka, taught me West Lake was easier drunk.

"He was your friend, not mine," Jeff said.

31

The line went dead.

I found Eric's obituary online: 42, dead 10-19-07. Strickland Funeral Home.

The drive back was snow, rust, and silence. West Lake had bled out its factories; those who stayed carried unemployment in their faces. Tug Hill was the same—decaying asphalt, stalled construction, ghosts in the weeds.

I'd first met Eric when his brother dented our screen door practicing wheelies. While our fathers shouted in the yard, Eric led me up an apple tree, sat me in a crook, and declared me his co-pilot.

"I've got a superhero hideout," he said, pointing at the telephone poles. "Between five and six, there's a trapdoor. You just have to believe."

He wanted to be anyone but himself.

I called Ronald Bulleri. The childhood bully with the pituitary tumor, built like an ape, an old scar riding his arm. Still in West Lake, wiping asses in a nursing home.

"Eric's dead," I told him.

"The fake superhero?"

"Are you going to the funeral?"

"Fuck that loser."

Some people never change.

It was June '87, last day of school. DJ, Jeff, and Ron were rowdy. Ronald had me on the ground, face in the gravel, when Eric stepped in—tracksuit, hood tight, red mask pulled over his face.

"Leave him alone."

They laughed, called him a freak. A rock split his lip, blood pouring through his hands.

Ronald sneered.

Eric ran.

We never saw him again.

Rumors said his father beat him into a coma. My mother said he'd gone to live with an aunt. Either way, high school started one kid short.

Older now, broken, hauling memories like wet newspapers, I walked Tug Hill, where the poles kept count. At pole five my hands shook, ash from the Marlboro spitting into the snow with a hiss. I clawed at the drift until metal caught—an old handle, worn smooth.

I hauled it up, opened the hatch, and slid into the dark, my boot hooking the ladder's first rung.

I hit concrete, the fall kicking the breath out of me—lungs seized, air trapped, the way it always was.

When I rose, the place sharpened: valves, tools, a sewer map ghosted under a dim bulb. Across the wall, a tracksuit and a red mask sagged like artifacts of a forgotten saint.

I dragged the old tracksuit over me, cloth straining, belly exposed, wrists bare. It fit like a memory, wrong in every place. The red mask sagged across my face. Rusted pipe in hand, cigarette burning through the fabric.

Headed toward Ronald Bulleri's house.

# THE UNKNOWN

Animals howl, humans cry out. The boy, because of his condition, did neither. His heart triggered the alarm: a shrill cry and a red light above the door. The nurse silenced it with a pudgy finger, never lifting her eyes from her phone.

He came to rehab after the accident unencumbered—no tubes, no pumps—only the cardiac leads pasted to his pale chest. His prognosis reduced to one word—unknown.

Staff spoke as if his consciousness lived only in alarms, though his body never moved.

His room sat at the hall's end, chlorine from the therapy pool mingling with lotions, balms, and the nicotine ferried in through a side door propped with a mop.

Across the hall, another family kept vigil—silence their only tongue, heavy as stone.

The first time his heart faltered, his mother was bent over granite in the lobby bathroom, snorting the last of her Oxy and Xanax. By the time she returned, the team had revived him.

A day later she slipped out to score more, and again the alarm blared. Powder rippled through her nasal tissue as she sensed, animal-like, that the boy needed her.

Before his accident, she'd lived on what she called a Cadillac High: pills, a nanny for the child, a husband soon gone. The Oxy began with a 30mg Blueberry pressed into her palm while movers loaded her ex's things.

She chased it through handbags, across pool decks, and finally into the parking lot of a pill mill, joining a half-circle of strangers feigning back pain.

By day three at her son's bedside, withdrawal had her trembling and fouling the bathroom floor. By day four she sweated through her clothes, bowels ungoverned. On day five, empty and raw, she listened to his heartbeat, slow and steady, and clung to it.

She found comfort in the routine: staff bending his limbs against contractures, laying bony prominences on pillows as if into coffins. Pinned by the unknown, she sipped coffee in the still moments, watched long-timers clutch Bibles, watched newcomers beg for miracles.

Sobriety brought memories back jagged: the unhappiness of her pregnancy, the infant who screamed himself blue, the marriage gone gray.

What she could not recover was the 911 call—the lights splitting her empty living room, EMS ignoring her as they worked the boy. The blanket draped across her shoulders, meant for comfort, covering her shame.

Over time—through alarms and sobriety—the boy drew her back. Back from the Cadillac high, the divorce, the pool night where her absence became his.

She sat with him, halo of blonde hair spilled on the pillow, and the ache of mothering settled in.

Knowing she could never leave—a penance—she looked into his eyes. In their blue shimmered a tacit covenant: savior and saved.

# NAKED BOY LEADS
# POLICE ON CHASE

The first time I fucked an older woman, I ended up in the morning news-paper. There I was, flat on my back, staring at my white athletic socks, while a woman with breasts like pendulums climbed atop me and rode out a moan, her towheaded toddler circling the bed as though the scene were ordinary.

The summer of '86 had delivered me to an Armenian nail polish factory on Twelfth Street. Sixteen, fulfilling probation for shoplifting at Miller's Market with my Tug Hill friends.

Picture the warehouse: a massive brick hulk that reeked of rat shit, acetone, and mold. On the second floor, a conveyor belt stretched forty feet, a metallic serpent lined with boxes of polishes named *Starter Wife*, *Jailbait*, *Espresso Your Style*. Around it, twelve of us capped bottles by hand, twelve-hour shifts that blistered my fingers so badly I could barely unbutton my Levi's to piss. Gloves, Vaseline, finger condoms — nothing dulled the pain.

Enter Mrs. Robinson. Yes, her real name. A line veteran. One day, as I squirmed with a full bladder, she leaned close.

"I'll get that for you," she said, unbuttoning my jeans with nimble fingers. I understood immediately: she wanted something in return.

I gave it. Gladly.

Soon I was on her couch in my best faux-leather jacket, Old Spice clinging to me. There were the triplets, diapered and wailing in their cribs, and the toddler, towheaded and curious, patrolling the edges of the bed where she stripped me naked and rode until spent. Our routine.

Weeks passed. The toddler grew comfortable enough to bang his empty bottle on my forehead like a plastic tomahawk. The game ended the day he shifted from shouting "milk, milk" to "Daddy, Daddy."

At first I thought he meant me. Then I saw his real father in the doorway, eyes wide, crossbow raised.

The first arrow buried itself in the headboard, inches from my ear.

"Donny!" Mrs. Robinson shouted. "Are you trying to kill the poor boy?"

"If I wanted to kill him—" he snapped, and loaded again.

I bolted, still hard, out the back door, bare ass flashing through the cut grass. Another arrow tore the frame as I dove into daylight, lungs full of terror, toes clutching earth for traction.

From the open window came the toddler's chant, bright as bells: "Daddy, Daddy."

Dispatch: 9-1-1 emergency.

Mrs. Robinson: I'm calling from 11 Snake Hill Road. My husband just chased a naked boy from the house with a crossbow.

Dispatch: Is anyone hurt?

Robinson: Not yet.

Dispatch: Can you see the boy?

Robinson: Uh-huh. He's in the neighbor's yard right now.

Dispatch: Can you see your husband?

Robinson: No, I'm in the kitchen.

I stole a bicycle from a garage two houses down. By the time squad cars descended, I was already a headline. *Naked Boy Leads Police on Chase.*

The charges stacked up: burglary, property damage, indecent exposure.

In court, the judge said, "Bond is $5,000. If he makes bond, he is not to appear in public unless fully clothed."

His gavel carried a leniency I didn't deserve.

"You could have been killed," he added, his eyes heavy on me.

"Just last month, a man shot his wife's lover at the Honey Spot Motor Lodge. Another stabbed a man in Suffolk. You were inches from the same fate."

I glanced back for Mr. Robinson, but he wasn't there. Just strangers filling the pews.

Mrs. Robinson sat in a corner, silent, eyes on the floor.

No one spoke of it outright. The silence lay heavy, even on the paper route, the news stiff in my hands.

Mrs. Robinson, they said, went back to the factory, to quieter habits. Life, eventually, steadied. Yet for years after, every erection carried the ghost of that day: the thwack of a crossbow, the sting of grass on bare skin, the cool earth grabbing at my toes as I ran for my life.

# I AM A WINNER

*"I lie to myself all the time.*
*But I never believe me."*— S.E. Hinton

SAMANTHA LIBIN, Fox News Correspondent: What we know right now is that—yes—it's climbed to a billion dollars. Just look at these lovely, smiling people behind me.

LIBIN: Sir, what did you get? Did you buy your ticket?
UNIDENTIFIED MALE: No speak English.
LIBIN: Oh—no speak English. Okay.
LIBIN (turns back to camera): He's just bought a ticket. He's hoping he'll win the Powerball. The camera pans out.
LIBIN: Every single person who walks into this store is buying tickets.
DAVID PEREZ (anchor, off-set): You're more likely to get hit by an asteroid, draw a royal flush, or get attacked by a shark than win the lottery.
LIBIN: We have so many hopeful people. I've never seen anything like it.
A middle-aged woman lifts a fan of tickets above her head.
UNIDENTIFIED WOMAN: My heart's exploding. I'm feeling lucky today.

LIBIN: So, David—despite the odds—there's still a line down the block. Praying for the billion-dollar dream.

I am a winner.

Dexter Cobb repeated it until the words turned into smooth skipping stones, clicking across a wide, dark lake. He squinted, inhaled, watched the stones bounce in the shape of a red ball over the pale gray sulci of his brain.

Exhale.

A heavy smile rose, doughy as bread. This was his gift: he could see his words as things.

Under the bathroom fluorescents he leaned into the mirror, liberated a stubborn blackhead, then kneaded his face into what he imagined was a Powerball smile.

The first hesitation of his life came in the delivery room—eighteen hours of his mother's ragged labor, the nineteenth hour finally pushing him out, pale and shellacked in vernix.

The second hesitation was his breathing. The nurse fitted a tiny mask over his mouth, squeezed rhythm into his lungs, pressed two fingers to the center of his chest. His father watched from the corner, mute as a coat rack, unsure whether what rose from the sterile tent—a bird-thin cry—was relief or regret.

Dexter grew into a soft-edged boy who blinked at the world from behind his own glass. Bikes and cul-de-sacs gave way to rooms he wouldn't leave. He graduated by accident.

"You have no agency," his father told him once, thinking back to that panicked first hour and whatever got starved of air.

At twenty-six he lived in a room of leftovers: a recliner with the foam tired and exposed, a spider plant shedding green suggestions, a houndstooth couch that had lost its geometry, a "sofa-sized" oil painting bought from a starving-artist sale at the Ramada. "Ocean scenes, mountain vistas—thousands in value!" the commercial had promised.

Dexter nudged the frame until it sat level. He smiled.

The picture still didn't make sense, but it was straight.

35 Rolling Meadows squatted on three ranks of brutalist block, a residence run by Residential Health Services—a company with a slogan about privilege and life-enhancing care.

The best houses had staff who showed up, who cooked, who measured pills into paper cups and waited to see each one swallowed. The worst recycled the same bodies through their shifts until you couldn't tell residents from employees.

Rolling Meadows leaned toward the latter. Alice the med tech drifted across the couch at odd angles, pockets sweet with pilfered Adderall and Klonopin. She'd been moved from a prior site for lap-dancing a wheelchair user while the others clapped.

Linda—a twenty-four-year-old pear with lipstick for armor—treated the bathroom like a battlefield. Tina Pethybridge, legally blind, trailed behind with her long white cane ticking the world into place.

Henry Weatherby, oldest resident, self-appointed "senior staff," managed his fears by staying in his room and writing incident reports no one read. And Charlie—thirty, epileptic, thin as a wire—moved hot and unprotected through his days.

That evening, soap-shiny and naked, Charlie burst into the kitchen with Linda in pursuit. Dexter caught him by the shoulders. Charlie slipped free and went down hard on the linoleum.

"Your shower time is over, bitch," Linda said, breath white and bright.

Tina's cane rapped doorframes like a metronome. In the living room, Alice's snore rattled.

By eight o'clock they gathered for meds. Alice drooled. Charlie produced a tube of antifungal and rubbed it into his palms, eyeing the nest of toes in a sock he'd chosen not to remove.

"Do my feet tonight, Dexter?"

"I'll pass."

"How about you take my seizure pill instead? Makes me sleepy. I want to watch the drawing."

Dexter watched him smear cream across the cracked heel. A small life, he thought. His. Charlie's. Everyone's. "No need to stay up," Dexter said. "I'm the winner."

Charlie lit up and flung his arms around him. Dexter felt something unfasten inside. It was time.

Seven minutes after eight, Dexter declared himself sole winner of the Powerball. In the breakfast nook he flashed his prize smile. It wasn't God, it wasn't Tony Robbins ("Live as if your prayers are already answered"), it wasn't fever. It was simple: from the moment his mother's water slipped onto the floral Congoleum in their blue Cape Cod and she said, Oh, shit, this little bastard is coming, his life had been a punchline.

Tonight it wouldn't be.

Charlie fluttered like the ruby-throated at the feeder. He peeled off a sock and scuttled into the hall, chanting, "Winner, winner, chicken dinner." His voice was muffled by the wood, foam bubbling at his lips as excitement jostled the seizure line.

Linda rose to the bait, filling the corridor with her body. Charlie caromed and kept going.

"What are you doing with the money?" she shouted at Dexter.

"Start with clothes. Your clothes are tragic. Haircut, teeth, girlfriend. Or a hooker. Or both. But girlfriend for sure."

Tina came tapping in the opposite direction, rat-a-tat-tat.

Charlie thumped on Henry's door. No answer.

Winner winner chicken dinner," he sang into the wood.

"Let's celebrate," Linda said. "Field trip."

House rules required two staff, prior approval. Alice snored. Dexter had keys.

He opened the office, took them, and everything that followed belonged to the kingdom of the unadvised.

They piled into the Econoline with RHS stenciled on the quarter panel. Linda licked a window and announced they were getting married at Mohegan Sun and she'd need five thousand in small bills. Tina perched in front, smoothing her short-waisted dress, hair fluffed for the first time in a decade. Charlie chattered behind Dexter, the electrical storm under his skull looking for a place to land.

McDonald's, then Wendy's. Forty-five dollars of fries and meat collapsing onto asphalt. Tina asked for beer. She had never drank, never been taken to dinner, never worn a dress that wasn't for church. She might have said the word date. Dexter felt her hand find his and stay.

Behind the Sheetz they drank a case of Heineken into the early morning. Charlie's chant softened to a thread: "Winner… Winner…"

A Peterbilt rumbled in. Linda found a ginger driver hauling pigs to slaughter. She climbed up, blew Dexter a kiss, extended a middle finger like a bouquet.

"Send me the money, baby," she sang. The truck hooted and took her away.

Tina, trained only in the topography of Rolling Meadows, wandered into darkness to find a bathroom and stepped wrong into a thirsty creek bed. When Dexter found her she was crouched strange, neck at an angle that disobeyed explanation. He tried her name twice, then a third time with the softness he had never used on anyone. The water kept speaking.

Back at the van, Charlie had ridden the edge into seizure. By the time Dexter turned him, his mouth was a foam dam. It broke too late. The stillness that followed was a mercy and an indictment.

Two hours passed in a shape that refused to be known.

He brought the van home at first light, parking across the street. He slid the side door and shouldered Charlie's weight. Around back, through the quiet kitchen, down the hall, into the room. He covered him and laid a hand on the sheet until his hand learned the cold.

Henry appeared in khakis that had slept standing up, clipboard clutched like a bible.

"I called the police," he said. "Where are the others?"

Dexter eased past him to the last door on the left. Recliner. Spider plant. Houndstooth. Ocean painting with a horizon that couldn't agree with itself. He shut the door and listened: distant sirens tattooed the morning.

In the mirror he searched the unhinged rooms of his head for the stones he could throw across water. I am a winner, he told the boy in the glass. The words tried to lift, then fell, heavy and stupid, onto the dresser. They lay there like coins you couldn't spend.

Outside, somewhere beyond the block and the lawn, a woman on television told a camera the odds meant nothing to people in lines that never ended. In here, the lines had ended exactly where they always did.

Dexter straightened the painting until it was level, then stood very still, waiting for the sirens to arrive, and for whatever would be named after they did.

# DANDELION

She called it Dandelion.

I didn't argue. I had brought her here. Naming it troubled me, but I had no right to protest.

Every spring, dandelions scatter themselves without permission, white heads bobbing across lawns, impossible to control.

She pulls a bundle from her trunk, smelling of rubber and motor oil. She spreads a knitted comforter on the hill. We kick off our shoes, let the grass lick at our ankles. The hill is steep, the blanket sliding, as though gravity itself wanted us gone.

The sun drifts in and out, half-committed, warming her skin when it lingers. She adjusts her sundress, fabric bunched, the promise beneath flashing like a dare.

I press my hand to her stomach, against the thin floral print. I wait for vibration, for proof of something. There is nothing.

Under the light she opens, like a plant coaxed from soil. A scar where a piercing once lived glints below her navel. I cannot picture a swollen belly; I picture only the flat midriff, unspoiled. I try not to imagine Dandelion at all.

Inside, the question grows sharp: is it worse to wish for death, or to take part in it? Either way, the universe is listening, taking notes.

On Tuesday we carried home remedies from the co-op: cinnamon, papaya, black and blue and red cohosh. A list that sounded less like medicine than an exotic recipe. On Wednesday night we swallowed the lot, trusting the blogs that had no answers.

By Friday we were lying still on the hill, hands locked. Children ran nearby, their laughter ringing. Bare feet slapped the field. A dog's hot breath dampened the air. Everything shouted: *we exist*.

She slid her panties down, checked with her fingers. Waiting for absence.

A dandelion begins as a closed tube. Days later, a white globe trembles into being. Ours might never open.

We kissed. Not passion. Obligation.

Her arm lay before me, pale, a faint blue vein climbing until it vanished into the muscle. Her chest rose, fell. I thought: she was once someone's dandelion.

The field around us swayed with them. Seeds loosened, floated past my face. I watched one lift, weightless, drift toward a new horizon. Free in ways I wasn't.

I wondered if ours had taken root already, if conditions in her body were too rich for escape. If left alone, it would grow a taproot, rob her blind from within.

Everyone says cutting blooms is useless. You have to dig out the root. Even then, the plant remembers. Nature is a sculptor that honors no shortcuts and does not forget.

# NO CANCER

"How do I look?"

"You look fine, honey."

"Fine, or motherly?"

"You look like a mom."

"Are you sure?"

"Yes. I'm sure."

Lillian Ratcliff fluttered around the nursery as if a butterfly had entered her body. She moved unopened diapers from shelf to shelf. She rearranged stuffed animals, adjusted the mobile, cracked the window to clear the paint smell.

"What if they don't approve us?" she asked.

"We'll be fine."

"How's our credit?"

"Solid."

"And the medical records?"

"Yes, dear."

"And the tax returns?"

"Uhm-huh."

"We'll be great parents, Lil."

✢ ✢ ✢

The building stood twenty minutes away, brick and concrete with Italian cornices, lilies blooming around its foundation. It looked more like a coastal villa than a clinic. They climbed granite steps hand in hand.

Inside: cast stone walls, pink marble, a chandelier heavy enough to crush them if it fell. The waiting room was filled with women who looked like Lillian. They accepted glasses of cucumber water from a blonde with perfect posture.

"Dr. Gideon will see you now."

The office was small. Two chairs, one computer, a plaque. Gideon was thirty at most. Perfect hair. Perfect teeth. A salesman's smile.

"Excited?" he asked.

"Yes," Lillian said, her voice brittle despite the water.

"Boy or girl?"

"Girl."

"Eyes?"

"Blue."

"Hair?"

"Blonde."

"Height?"

"Five ten."

He typed each word slowly, as though chiseling. Then opened their records. "Aunt with dementia. Father, cardiovascular disease. Brother, colon cancer. Sister, breast cancer. Psychiatric illness." Each diagnosis was a stone dropped into the room.

Her husband shrank under the weight.

"We can adjust," Gideon said. "Crispr allows precision. But insurance won't cover both aesthetics and disease prevention. There isn't money for everything you want."

Lillian dug her heels into the carpet. "What does that mean?"

"Compromise," Gideon said. "Blue eyes or no cancer. Blonde hair or a healthy heart. You choose."

Her husband forced a hopeful smile. "Lil, we can make this work. A healthy baby—"

She rose, her face darkening. "I won't compromise. My mother told me not to marry flawed genes. And I didn't listen."

Sensing collapse, Gideon slipped from the room.

Her husband reached for her. "We could do it the old way. Save the money. Love whatever comes."

"Natural conception is barbaric," she snapped. "Do you want us laughed at? The only family with an inferior child?"

When Gideon returned, both were silent. She folded in on herself. He wilted beside her.

"Any progress?" Gideon asked.

Lillian burst past him, gone.

Her husband lingered. "We had a name. Annabelle." He whispered it like something already lost.

"A beautiful choice," Gideon said, his teeth gleaming.

✛   ✛   ✛

Weeks later, Lillian drove alone. One eye on the road, the other on a clear vial of semen packed in ice. Ninety miles, ending at a strip mall lined with discount stores and phone shops. A small sign read: *The Fertility Institute*.

Inside, a Kazakh biologist greeted her.

"In your country, I don't understand the high cost of designer babies," he said in near-perfect English.

"I edited my children, and my grandchildren, for a fraction."

He spun his monitor. Rows of stock-photo children appeared — medals, trophies, diplomas, staged perfection.

"They all look so perfect," Lillian whispered.

The biologist grinned. "What did you expect? Monsters?"

# ZERO

Father wore clothes that said, *I am responsible.*

Mother wore defiance.

Inside the courtroom the adjudicator arranged beds and after-school pickups. Work histories, credit scores, social media, $Q$ ratings. Twenty minutes in all.

The judge tapped his pen like a metronome, lifted his glasses, and spoke: "In the best interest of the children—custody to the mother. Father will be non-custodial."

Disbelief stole Father's tongue.

✛ ✛ ✛

A month later, the first exchange. Sunday noon, Mt. Moriah Church parking lot. Across the street Popeyes vented grease into Jesus's vestibule.

The night before, Father dreamed his children. They rose from vapor, pressed to his ribs, sobbing into his chest. His arms tightened until they shimmered away, leaving him with longing too large to measure and a grip that could not let go, the kind of grip that lives in your marrow, that bends your spine forward in grocery aisles and sends you scanning every playground, as if by sheer will you might conjure them back into your arms.

Father arrived early, brushing crumbs from the seat, pressing wrinkles flat with wet palms. Divorce had emptied his knowledge of parenting. He felt as new as the day his children were born.

Mother came late, cutting through the reverence of noon parishioners with frantic hands. Eldest live-streamed the swap, luggage passed trunk to trunk, Youngest and Eldest mumbling beneath Mother's steady monologue.

"The $Q$ loves angst," Eldest said.

Mother smiled. Father lowered his eyes.

"Gets it honest," she replied.

People lost their way—no way to measure their worth. Before the $Q$, you lived on likes and emojis. Digital applause, hollow as air. It seemed enough, until it wasn't.

The gap widened: smiles posted, wrists hidden. Then suicides— one, then another, then a wave. Famous founders. Anonymous housewives. Mid-life fathers in their garages.

The $Q$ promised something different: not a tally, but a universal rating—final, unambiguous—the new currency of worth. To earn it, you had to strip yourself bare: sharing, vulnerable, raw

These were the arguments before the divorce, scored not in words but in $Q$.

"Your $Q$ matters," Mother said.

"Bullshit," Father said. "I won't strip my life bare for strangers."

Her $Q$ sagged, lowest in the subdivision.

She painted her face, reddened her skin with her own hand, streamed tears.

"Father beat me."

Her $Q$ soared. She filed. The children learned.

✣ ✣ ✣

Weekends became rehearsals. Words trimmed for confession. Affection rationed for effect.

"Drop the *Q*," Father pleaded.

They stared.

"Just because you won't share doesn't mean we can't. Sharing might save you."

Youngest tapped his name into the app.

Zero.

"You don't exist," they said.

After they left, Father faced the mirror: collarbones like blades beneath his shirt, face narrowing into absence.

"Fuck the *Q*."

He ran. Around the block. Into the park. Sweat shining in moonlight. Urine dark. Breath tearing his chest. He ran until dawn bent him double, body slackened, lungs raw, and in that collapse he felt every failure accumulate—missed birthdays, silences at the dinner table, arguments that unraveled into paperwork—until the whole weight of his fatherhood pressed down like a final, unpayable debt.

"It's my weekend," Father begged. "I'll try," Mother said, already gone.

Only Youngest agreed. A single frayed thread.

**911 Transcript**
Incident 07-27541
October 19, 2020
13:02:02
Operator: 911.
Caller: My dad has a gun.
Operator: Anyone hurt?

Caller: Not yet.
Operator: Where are you?
Caller: Wilborn Avenue.
Operator: Name?
Caller: Eldest. My sister's here too.
Operator: Is she safe?
Caller: For now. But Father—

Negotiator: Do you have a gun?
Father: Wrong house. No danger.
Negotiator: Let's get your kids safe.
Father: They're upset. Not in danger.
Negotiator: It's been hard. We can talk.
Father: Leave me the fuck alone.

**911 Transcript**
13:22:07
Caller: He's coming—he's screaming—help—don't—
**End Transcript**

**Local Bulletin**
Posted Oct 20, 2020
LOCAL—Police shot and killed a man during a standoff. Divorce and custody loss cited as motives.
"The safety of our citizens is paramount," said the lieutenant.
Eldest told reporters: "We're just glad we're safe." Their stream drew millions.
The mayor praised them.
"A heroic *Q* share," he said.
And you nodded. Because you were watching. Because you, too, need the *Q*.

And somewhere, behind the applause and the headlines, a father's silence hangs like smoke in a closed room, thick enough to taste, impossible to clear.

# THE SIGNAL
# NEVER ENDS

I'm a motionless, corpulent statue in my yard. Caramel-colored leaves skitter between my feet. Sugar maple, loblolly pine, sweetgum bleeding red. Since the accident I've become an amateur arborist, thanks to the Nature Channel. Naming the trees helps pass the time.

My head tilts twenty degrees to catch the satellite. Dish on the deck, beam from space, my skull the bridge between them. At first, it was agony—nausea, vertigo, a roar in the ears. Now I've learned to manage.

For weeks, I've been downloading DirecTV straight into my brain. No contract. No receiver. A gift. Or theft. Depends on your view.

It began after I fell from a ladder while painting the barn. Eight feet, grass landing. A headache came on, then deepened. At urgent care, the doctor gave me oxycodone, a work note, and this advice: *Rest your brain.*

Instead, I wandered into the yard, stepped between the dish and the sky, and felt the first surge—like an intellectual orgasm. I'm no genius, but I knew microwave signals could scramble a brain. In me, they opened a gate. Programming rushed in. Cooking shows, rehab shows, pornography. My head filled with channels.

Now I'm a different man. I tackle my daughter's homework in minutes. I cook orecchiette with pancetta and pumpkin. Two weeks ago, I couldn't boil water.

My wife smiles more. She tells me sex has never been better. Two, three times a day, curiosity renewed. She says "better," but not "I love you." That part disturbs me.

At night I tuck my daughter in with fairy tales pulled from a children's show lodged in my skull. She falls asleep smiling. My wife waits in the bedroom. When she's finished with me, I slip outside, position myself back between dish and sky, and stay until dawn.

✢ ✢ ✢

But the signal crowds out the old me. I'm forgetting the man I was. At the grocery store I tried to pay in the cadence of an infomercial.

"Two easy payments of $19.99," I told the clerk. He reached for the phone.

"But wait, there's more!" I shouted as I shoved my way out.

Storms from the Caribbean sometimes knock the signal out. During those hours, life feels almost normal. Rain on the roof. My wife shopping on her iPad. My daughter close at the table. I trace a finger down my wife's neck until she moans, natural this time. We kiss like we used to.

"It's better this way," I whisper. "Let life return to normal."

The screen flickers. *No signal* blinks, then returns. The strobe of lost-and-found light paints the room. We kiss again.

She smiles. "I'll be right back."

When she returns, she carries my raincoat. She slips it onto my shoulders, kisses my forehead, and guides me gently to the back door.

"The signal will be back any minute," she says.

Outside, the night is thick. I look for the sweetgums bleeding red, but the dark has swallowed them.

Then came my wife's voice, faint but clear—high, tinny, distorted. She was laughing. I couldn't see her, only hear her, as if she existed now only in sound. Through the static I realized: she was coming to me on the signal. And the signal never ends.

# THE BOX DID WHAT
# BOXES DO

### *Twelve Hours*

"It's such an honor," Grace said, humming as she crossed the kitchen floor. After sixteen years of marriage, she was still stunning, still using her harmonic hum to probe my emotional temperature for annoyance.

"Yes," I said. "An honor."

The black box sat on the table, its lore pressed into ninety-degree edges. As children we were told of the unimaginable suffering before the box: my grandfather to my father, my father to me, me to my daughter.

It had arrived minutes ago, wrapped in silence, a twelve-hour countdown stamped in gold. Our name — Nixon — embossed on the top. From the beginning we had decided: if a box ever came, I would be the one responsible for its contents.

"See you tonight," Grace said, kissing the corner of my forced smile before sending me out the door.

### *Eight hours, twelve minutes*

On the light rail, people whispered. At the office my coworkers popped from cubicles like whack-a-mole, then ducked back after my soft thank-you. Their relief sat behind their teeth, unspeakable: *Thank God it wasn't us.*

No one asked the real questions. Could the box be buried? Ignored? What if you refused? Instead: Was it heavy? Did the gold lettering shine?

At noon there was cake. Alice in HR had baked it in the shape of an hourglass, no sand remaining, gold fondant borders. Joyce from accounting and I stood in the center as everyone clapped. She beamed. I winced. Acid stripped my throat raw.

## Four hours, seven minutes

On the train home I thought about my yard. The paint peeling from the porch, the crooked shutters, the broken spindles. In my head I kept hammering repairs I would never make.

In the driveway, the smell of cut grass pulled me back. I gripped the doorknob with an unsteady hand.

"Honey, I'm home." A phrase I'd never used in twenty-two years of marriage, compelled now to play the part.

Inside: a swell of hugs and handshakes. A pulpous swarm. Flesh pressing, smiles too wide. I shrank, afraid they would notice.

## Three hours

The charade collapsed quickly. My body slumped on the couch, a plate untouched in my lap. Abby sat beside me with nachos, cheese running down her chin. She offered me lemonade.

## Two hours

"It was worse before the box," she said.
"Yes."

"They fixed it."

"They controlled it."

Something in my voice cracked. She stiffened.

"People are happier now," she said, chewing noisily.

I folded into myself, then blurted: "I don't think I can do it." My hands gripped her knees like a beggar.

She pulled back, eyes sharp.

"What do you mean?"

## One hour

"It's wrong," I whispered. My wife was outside, wrestling the swollen trash bin.

"It's your responsibility." Abby's voice broke. "It's the law. Do you want things to go back?"

Images spilled from her mouth — food riots, thirst, endless queues. The horrors of before.

"No," I said.

"You've always told me: we gain from loss."

## Ten minutes

I thought of my rehearsed line. Eight words I believed could save me. I gambled them.

"Do you know how much I love you?"

For a moment she was silent, her face unreadable, the kitchen lit by ordinary lamplight, my wife's clatter in the background. Then Abby spoke flatly, like her mother:

"Daddy, it's your day. We've celebrated."

Her words torpedoed my courage. Shame dragged me down.

She turned her gaze to the box. She had only ever known one existence, one way of life.

"Don't make me ashamed of you."

Then she was gone. The door shut behind her.

The black box sat alone on the kitchen table, edges sharp, my name embossed in gold.

## *Zero*

The countdown blinked. The numbers dissolved into nothing.

The lid opened with a sigh, soft as breath. Inside, the darkness waited.

I reached in and felt its teeth.

And the box did what boxes do.

# THE DEAD LINE

I've disappointed everyone.

It's written into the A-C-G-T of my DNA. Depending on our relationship, your disappointment might range from mild frustration to abject regret. If I haven't disappointed you yet, give it time.

Please don't rob me of the grandeur of my destruction. Normalcy is a gift, but it never holds. Choices decay, collapse into catastrophe.

✢ ✢ ✢

My days repeat. Breakfast: stale cereal, Jack Daniels. The need to escape grows until I leave my apartment.

At the co-op, I slump against the wall. That's when she appears — her torso hidden in a payphone booth, her legs visible beneath the half-glass. Her dress clenched in her fist, fabric drawn high, exposing pale thigh.

Her mouth twists under the weight of words meant for someone else. She looks up, finds me staring. Eyes like tacks. A shrug, a flip of hair into sunlight. Shadows scatter across her freckled chest, damp with sweat.

She closes the distance. "I need a ride."

"Yes," I say, though doubt curls in my throat.

We drive through dusk. She directs me to a narrow house. Inside, thin bodies huddle in corners like rats for warmth. She disappears down a hallway. Voices rise, faceless.

When she returns, her fingers are stained with oil, balancing foil and pipe. Afghan hash. I don't resist. Smoke sears my throat, lifts me from the couch. I rise above the room, above myself.

Morning burns me back into the world. My arms drape the sofa. Pants tangled at my ankles, cock limp, mouth dry as powder. A bottle of Jim Beam between my feet.

She's gone. So are my wallet, phone, and keys.

I stagger outside, stop an old man on the broken sidewalk. His lips chalky, spittle caked at the corners.

"What day?" I ask. He mutters, brushes past.

Days later, the sting still blooms. I return to the co-op, wait among strangers. Shuffle faces like cards in a deck. Hours slip.

Then she reappears — hair catching light, fingers drawing fabric high. Another man watches, hungry, already following her.

I push through the crowd, lose them, and end at the payphone. Receiver in hand.

The cord dangles loose. The line is dead.

# SEVEN DAYS WITH THE DEVIL

## Day 1

My days are dull, lifeless, interchangeable.

On a bare mattress, eyes fixed to the ceiling, I smoke a blunt. The night drinks the smoke. Rain weighs the leaves. Crickets fall silent. A lamp sputters, buzzes, dies.

Addiction. Loneliness. Wanting to be alone. A desire for resurrection.

I decide to try. At the Troy Goodwill I buy a Dirt Devil® mop. A week of redemption: clean the floors, smoke the rest of my stash, start again.

The mop is smooth plastic, red and reassuring. I push it across the kitchen, the bathroom. Each pass strips something away. For once, it works.

At night I smoke again, exhale through a straw salvaged from take-out. Under haze, the mop glows in the corner. I drift.

## Day 2

I wake at noon, the air conditioner coughing its last. Rent's late; complaining pointless.

I hit the hash, then the floors. Roaches scatter. I empty the sink. Bills pile the table; I sweep them into the trash, except for one letter.

## Day 3

For once I rise before smoking. The mop stands upright, smug.

I shower, re-wear dirty clothes, walk the block. Dinner is old Thai noodles. The night passes quietly.

## Day 4

I wake with a dull knock in my head. Toss moldy food. Sort laundry by color. Begin a job application, abandon it halfway.

In the afternoon I light up. The mop feels foreign, almost resentful. Steam rises, the knock grows sharper.

On the table, the letter waits.

*Hey, #1 Grandson,*

*No word from you in a while. I imagine what you're going through. Summer was hot here, now it's cool. I quit the garage; boring days. The store down the street is going up fast. Traffic forever. Sam tried a scam with the Realty people, lost a third of his property's value. Greedy Gus. Anyway, write when you can. Calls aren't the same. I'm sending a little change I saved for you.*

*Love, Grandma and Grandpa*

Tears come. Another hit dulls them. My supply shrinks, but I smoke less. Progress, I tell myself.

# Day 5

I sleep late. The mop watches me. I throw a shoe, miss.

Fuck cleaning. I smoke until the day dissolves. Ants trace a black line along the baseboard. I follow them for hours until darkness takes me.

# Day 6

I crawl to the couch. Smoke with crusted eyes. There's no one left to blame. Just me. Just a mop.

Cleanliness is no salvation. The stash is almost gone. The floors dull again. Roaches return, triumphant. My life is an Etch-A-Sketch — every effort shaken blank.

I once read: misguided good men are more dangerous than motivated bad ones. I feel misguided, kneeling to an appliance.

# Day 7

I pace the apartment, the knock in my skull now a drum. The mop sneers from the corner.

"No more!" I shout, jerking the cord tight. The casing cracks — a cheap plastic skull splitting open — and the shards bite into my wrist. The artery bursts. Blood pulses across the floor as I stagger for the door.

I slam it wide, rebound into my forehead. Dizzy, I whirl, shot-put the mop into the morning air. The cord whips behind it like a tail.

Mid-throw, regret stabs me. Too late.

The Devil smashes against a concrete divider, body spinning, plastic cracking.

For a moment, the world sharpens.

Bare feet find the asphalt. The sun blinds me at the threshold. I step into the parking lot, my blood emptying onto the dark.

Free.

# PHANTOM BEACH

My ex-girlfriend's cat's Meloxicam tasted bitter, chemical. But I've swallowed worse. As addicts go, I've cycled through the basics — booze, hash, opioids, pills, powders, tabs. Nothing holds a candle to my current addiction.

Friday night, I take my girlfriend to dinner. She grouses about a Facebook friend's drama. I nod, thinking of the past eleven months: dating, sex, families, cohabitation. All the stages ticked.

✛ ✛ ✛

The appetizers arrive when my phone buzzes. She stiffens. We fought yesterday, so she swallows her words. Her blouse catches a splash of Merlot. The waiter leans in, blotting her breast with his napkin. Fingers linger on the silk.

I should care. I don't. I'm already elsewhere.

@girl_wanderlust has posted again. I scroll past the thong shot, stop on a hiking photo. Ball cap, shorts, T-shirt — better. She has half a million likes, strangers calling her "delicious."

Under the table, muscle memory takes over: thumbprint, tap, scroll. The same way amputees feel phantom limbs. My addiction erodes the subconscious.

Instagram is my heroin.

Dinner arrives. Cold broccoli, pale and limp. I cover it with a napkin as if it's a corpse. My girlfriend flirts with the waiter. I sink back into the feed.

I'm in a jungle. Parrots shriek, thorns gouge. I follow her down a rutted path into a fishing village, music thumping from a shack. Gulls caw overhead.

A tap on my shoulder.

"Cash or card?"

The waiter stands over me, bill folder in hand.

I surface. The jungle dissolves. My girlfriend drops her eyes. I hand him my card. We leave.

She drives home fast. Car door slams. Apartment door slams. Bedroom door slams. The lock clicks.

I don't knock. I go to the bathroom. Time for a fix.

The stink of my own urine finally pulls me back from the feed.

Hours later I crawl into bed. "I thought you pulled an Elvis," she mumbles.

"Not dead on the toilet. Just reading."

"For five hours?"

"That long?"

A scrap flares, dies like wet firewood.

At dawn, I grope for my phone. Salvation. @girl_wanderlust posted again.

The bed dissolves. I'm waist-deep in the Caribbean, water slipping through my fingers. Onshore, a hammock sways. She waits.

"Where do you go?" My girlfriend shakes me. The ocean, hut, iguana vanish. "You need to stay off your phone."

I promise a week without it. A peace offering tossed into the fridge.

I last half a day.

After pity sex, I dig the phone out from behind the eggs. Back to her world: hardwood floors, a summer porch, her naked in a kitchen spilling wine.

A sudden drop — guillotine clean. The screen goes black.

She's standing over me, phone in hand.

"Who is this? You know she doesn't know you exist? I'm right here. A living, breathing person. And you're addicted to a stranger."

Her voice cracks. The phone slams against the counter, screen splintering.

"I'm leaving," she says. The door slams. Shock waves ricochet.

I shove my hands into my pockets. Sand grits my fingertips. Moist grains. The phantom beach. I rub the residue, smell the ocean.

And scroll.

# LOVE M

Menopause is a provocative convergence: a queer loss of genital plea-sure, of reproductive purpose, of self. As with most, Mother's contracted fertility didn't come to a sudden stop. It dwindled. A slow, hormonal burn that aborted her purpose.

A botanist by profession, Mother understood the climacteric; the physiological changes that marked the end of fruit maturation and the onset of senescence. Mother said her fruit was rotten. She was 49.

She attempted to mitigate the effects and sought needful things to love and nurture. Adopted armfuls of shelter cats. Dozens of tropical house plants. Ficus, elephant's ear, Boston ferns, unpruned. Her apart-ment became a strange scrub of fronds and small carnivorous mammals.

✛ ✛ ✛

Mother gave me more than half her diminutive DNA. She gifted a shared impotence built upon a faulty existence and fractured relation-ships. We attempted to renew family bonds. But my aunts, uncles, cous-ins—her siblings and my father, her ex—kept their distance as Mother mismanaged the consequences of her aging, and I, my sexuality.

"There's Little Miss Menopause and her pocket gay," they said.

Thus, I became a placeholder for Mother's next tragedy and gained an unwanted insight into her thorny melancholy.

Every Wednesday, we had lunch. A local café. At our most recent outing, amongst uneaten pasta, Mother arched toward the sunlight.

"I am worthless."

"Not worthless," I said.

"It's a terrible thing to expire."

"You're not expired."

"Worthless," she repeated.

"You have cats; they need you."

"They don't. Cats need no one."

This was lunch. Serve and volley.

"Open a nursery. You love plants."

"Too much work," she said.

I didn't argue.

Rooted in languid ambition, the simplest acts overwhelmed her. Her mawkish desperation bored a pit in my stomach as her essence faded into foliage and fur.

In late August, during the violent throes of menopause, she turned her attention to a killer whale. A solo female who languished in the Salish Sea. Mother mapped the whale's movements on her kitchen table in thick red marker.

On live TV, the grieving orca nudged the body of her dead calf into an estuary. When the calf drifted, the orca dove and lifted it again, lifeless and pale, with her nose. Daily, the rough waters chopped away at her efforts until starvation loomed.

Mother sobbed. The nation held its breath. Orcaholics stood vigil under gray skies. Scientists gathered. Social media exploded.

A local biologist reported that a killer whale without a pod is solitary, unique, sad. Mother identified with Lucy's plight.

"I can spot her by the slope of her dorsal fin," she said as the camera panned. CNN plastered "Lucy's tour of grief" across the screen.

Days before she disappeared, her words took on a giddy lightness. She told me that three known mammals experienced menopause: the killer whale, the pilot whale, and the human female. She paralleled her post-mothering trajectory with that of the sophisticated mammal.

"There's a mother's connection," she said.

"With whom?"

"Lucy."

The following week, she missed our lunch. Never called. Never texted. That evening, I searched her apartment and found only emptiness.

She left breadcrumbs: orca clippings on the wall, her map, a scatter of postcards, and a new buoyancy in her voice. She spoke of purpose. Of serendipity.

We lived outside Goose Prairie, Washington. An hour into my search I pulled off SR 410W, sent a barrage of texts. No reply.

On the dashboard, a handful of postcards: Naches Tavern. Each signed, *Love M.*

When Mother spoke of Naches' Tavern, she spoke of wildness. Of salvation. A parental imperative laced her words: "No matter what, you must stop."

"A pilgrimage?" I asked.

"Of sorts," she said.

I drove west as the peaks of Rainier loomed. Childhood memories of Appalachia and Carolina buffered the loneliness. Easterners by birth, Mother and I had always fought the depressive topography. After the divorce, my family split the country: Maine and Washington State. Few points more distant.

Weary hikers crowded the parking lot of the rustic dive bar. A handful of Harleys leaned front row. Travelers swapped stories on the porch.

Inside, a tall man with gray hair pulled into a ponytail worked behind the bar.

"I'm Mac," he said. "Here if you need me."

As the night thinned, he poured me another. Whiskey, smoke, flannel damp with sweat. He said the tavern was his second love.

The night blurred. Hands rough on my hips. Denim against skin. Stubble, tongue, silence. A body pressed hard against mine until everything broke loose.

After, he slid me water, cracked Advil into his palm. The kitchen clattered with knives. I pushed a postcard across the counter, Mother's scrawl fresh in my mind.

"You're M," I said. "You loved my mother."

He didn't look up. "We loved each other," he said.

"But for reasons you might now understand, I needed something different."

The car rose through Chinook Pass, past glaciers and jagged peaks. Enumclaw. Greenwater. I stopped for coffee, texted Mother again. No reply.

By noon I reached Puget Sound. Alki Point. A crowd gathered with binoculars, waiting for the whale. Flyers cried: *The whales are starving. We are killing them.*

And then she appeared. My mother. At the overlook, stripped bare. Hair loose, arms wide, her body pale against the sky. The crowd gasped.

She turned, smiled, and without pause, leapt.

In the water she swam toward the orca, grunting against the chop. Beside the dead calf she steadied herself, buoyed the carcass, gave Lucy a moment of rest. The whale exhaled, spraying a rainbow into the rain. The crowd cheered.

I saw her fist rise from the waves, clenched, defiant. A signal: she was still here. Still relevant. And in that instant, so was I.

# PALMAR ENTRAPMENT SYNDROME

"Nomophobia."

No response.

"NO Mobile PHOne phoBIA," Carr snapped.

The kiosk whirred, metallic skin shifting. Carr shuffled back.

To his right, a woman with a Samsung fused to her hand wrestled with the payment portal. Beyond her, a bus emptied, new arrivals shuffling in clouds of gravel dust. Most clutched their devices like holy relics. A few raised selfie sticks. The bus groaned away, leaving the faint haze of a carbon scrubber in the distance.

Carr stared at the rubber peeling from his Converse. Then the kiosk found him.

"Congratulations, Kenneth Carr. Thank you for choosing Recovery Works for your addiction."

He winced at "recovery," at "addiction." Those were for drug users. Real addicts. Not him.

"Please accept the terms of your rehabilitation."

"I accept."

The door hissed. Carr stepped into the pod.

The voice was mechanical, female. "Remove your clothing. Dress in the gown provided."

He stripped. A drawer slid open; he placed his clothes inside.

"Place your left hand into the aperture."

His iPhone was still fused to the palm. He slid his hand into the steel opening. Coolness flooded his arm. Relief. For the first time in months, silence from the endless buzzing.

A blade. The sudden numbness. The cautery smell of burnt flesh.

His hand, with the iPhone attached, landed in a bucket with dozens of others.

Three days earlier, he'd been on the brown sofa, his wife Bethany staring at him, her mother rigid in the recliner. He'd perched on the footrest between them, his phone welded to his hand.

They spoke of options. He stared at the carpet stains, remembering when he and Bethany fucked there—before the phone hollowed him out.

"I can change," he'd said.

"You're no good to me like this," Bethany replied.

Her mother folded her arms: "Last chance."

Carr had tried. Towels wrapped around his hand at night. Steroid injections. Solvents, adhesive removers, gimmicks ordered online. A hammer and chisel, one drunken night. The doctor finally gave the verdict: *Rehab might be your best option.*

Palmar Entrapment Syndrome. PES. Clinics multiplied — strip malls, luxury desert spas, names like NuLife Recovery and Eternal Springs. And so, Bakersfield. Insurance-covered. Non-negotiable.

Two days into the pod, Carr's hand throbbed. He shouted at the walls.

"You cut off my fucking hand."

The camera eye blinked red. "Did you not read the terms and conditions, Kenneth Carr?"

Pain pills clinked into the drawer.

By the third day, tremors. Sweat soaked the white gown, staining it gray. His stomach knotted around boluses of tasteless carbs.

Bethany appeared in the haze. Her arms dangled past her knees.

"How long have you neglected me?" she asked.

"I love you," he said.

Her face sloughed, exposing steel. Blood — or grease, or dirt — smeared across the floor where her hands dragged.

"How long?"

He woke pressed to the wall, whispering pleas into the speaker grille. The camera bathed him in red light, scanning him like rotten produce at a supermarket till.

"Do you love your wife, Kenneth Carr?"

"What?"

"Excessive technology use leads you away from those you love."

The pauses felt like judgment.

By morning, the walls crawled with words — his searches, his messages, his comments. Symbols replicating like damaged DNA. They spread across his gown, crawled into his eyelids.

Claustrophobic, he inhaled them. His own words filling his lungs.

None of this was his fault. "They make them this way," he muttered. "To take over your mind."

At ninety-six hours, the pod door opened.

"Always remember: connect with life, not your device."

Carr stepped into the afternoon sun. A breeze carried soot from the smokestack. A fleck landed in his palm.

He rubbed it between his fingers, wondering if it was part of his former self.

# SHIFT WORK

**7:38 a.m.**

On a desk bolted to the floor, a day-old sandwich soaks in spilled chocolate milk. The window above eye level is crisscrossed with wire. Here Willie languishes. Twenty years without a word beyond a grunt. A crusted old man with deep-set eyes and a sagging jaw.

"Time to move, Willie." I jab his kidney. He yelps like an animal. I tell myself it's motivation.

Today is cleaning day. Once a week the residents are herded out while housekeeping floods the unit with bleach. While the floors dry, Willie butts his head against the locked door, waits out the chemicals, then slips back inside.

**11:13 a.m.**

Patsy Dolan jerks and twitches, sounds tumbling from her throat — half grunts, half words. Huntington's stripped her body of control, but left her rage intact.

"Hello, Patsy," I say, stepping in her path. Her St. Vitus' dance arms whirl from Huntington's — one catches me square, cracks my nose. Blood trickles. She stammers an apology. I smirk and call a Code 5.

Nurses swarm. Patsy thrashes until leather straps pin her to the bed.

## 14:01 p.m.

Catherine Toth chain-smokes like the world depends on it. At twenty-eight she had a husband and two daughters. Now she is a hypersexual psychotic, her family ghosted in smoke.

During visitation she rocks while her oldest waves away the haze. The baby screams. Catherine lights another. Her husband gathers the children and flees.

Back on the stairs, our routine: I unbuckle, she unbuttons. On her knees until I finish. Payment is a bag of cigarette butts scooped from the ashtray.

## 15:07 p.m.

Day staff bustle before shift change. From behind the fishbowl, a nurse mouths, *Free Patsy*. I wave her off. Not her call.

In the smoking room, Willie drools in the corner beside Catherine. I bark, they flinch apart. I mark my sheet and move on.

## 16:00 p.m.

Near shift's end, I finally go to Patsy's room. She flops on the bed, eyes wild. Two steps inside, pain bursts at my skull. My bladder empties.

When I surface, Catherine is stripping my shoes, my pants. She's naked. Patsy claws my face, ripping flesh, grinning.

"What the hell are you doing?"

Catherine lowers herself onto me, rocking until I harden. Patsy screeches and digs at my skin. I fight the straps, screaming.

From the darkness, Willie leans close. His jaw slack, drool stringing his lip.

"Cleaning day," he whispers.

# I DON'T NEED THEM

I should have turned back. Instead, I rang the bell.

"Ms. Calder?"

Through the crack, she fiddled with the buttons of her white shirt, fingers brushing her throat. Her body swayed in the doorway, a pendulum in the silence.

"There's no pressure," I said.

She sighed, rigid smile softening. "No, please. I'm ready."

The email had arrived less than twelve hours earlier:

*James,*

*I am desperate to hire a film photographer.*
*I'll triple your standard fee. This is urgent.*
*—Elizabeth Calder*

Fifteen hundred dollars. Two months behind on child support. Debt mounting. I told her 11:00 a.m.

✛ ✛ ✛

The house was an immaculate Victorian in Wilmington, fronted with magnolias and shut off by an iron gate. Not my usual clientele.

"Is there anyone else home?" I asked.

"No, my husband's at work. Can we get started?"

She led me to her husband's office. Floor-to-ceiling books, dark leather chairs, a mahogany desk. Before I could comment, she stripped.

Shirt, pants, all of it gone in seconds. The transformation was surgical: proper woman to nude stranger.

"I need my entire body photographed," she said, eyes locked on mine.

"Can you do it?"

"Yes," I managed. "Though never quite this way."

I unpacked the camera. Checked light. Snapped a test. Without a word, she rotated—quarter turn, another, another. Like clock hands. Each angle offered, received, recorded.

Fifteen minutes. Twenty-two frames. She dressed with the same mechanical precision. Handed me the bills. Her palm touched my elbow, guiding me to the door.

"When do you need them?" I asked. "Tomorrow?"

"Yes... tomorrow."

The door shut.

That night I processed the film. Reel to developer. Stop bath to fixer. Hung to dry under the red safelight.

At first I thought it was contamination: splotches, blemishes. But as the images emerged, so did the truth.

Her skin was a map of violence.

Bruises bloomed across breasts and hips. Welts rose along her back. Scrapes striped her throat and face. Bite marks, dozens of them, stippled her arms and thighs.

I printed again. Glossy. Matte. Cropped. Enlarged. The damage never vanished. It only sharpened.

By dawn, my stomach burned acid. Twenty-two photographs lay on my desk. I gathered them, grabbed my coat, and drove back to Wilmington.

The gate loomed. I circled until I found parking, waited until my hands stopped shaking, then rang the bell.

A well-dressed blonde opened the door. "Can I help you?"

"I'm here to see Elizabeth Calder."

She blinked. "I'm sorry. Elizabeth passed away years ago."

Her hand rose to her arm, fingers kneading a fresh bruise.

I checked the number.

"No, that can't be right."

"My name is Mrs. Dean. Elizabeth was my husband's first wife. Today's the anniversary of her death."

Exits turned in my head: excuse myself, leave, run. Instead I froze on the step, the photographs burning a hole in my coat.

I walked away, but my legs carried me back, as if they belonged to someone else. I held out the envelope.

My voice cracked like a confession.

"I believe these are for you."

She thumbed the flap, shuffled the photos, then let her hand drop.

# FAIRVIEW

## 1

"Empty the register!"

The shout cracked across the aisles of Spam and dusty instant meals. A customer shrieked, knocking pork rinds into the air. The corner drunk pressed his belly against the beer cooler. Others scuttled into the stock room, roaches under light. The gunman tugged his hoodie tight.

Outside, the OPEN sign flickered, the awning sagged, trash piled, an abandoned car rusted. This corner store had always been easy prey: cash on hand, tired clerks, weak locks. But it was where Fairview lived — the day drinkers, stoners, shift workers, the broke, the left behind.

## 2

The gunman's eyes darted. His scowl knotted, a twitch jumping in his left eye. Fear and defiance braided in his voice. He side-eyed the drunk plastered to the cooler.

"We are being robbed!" the drunk shouted, slurring the obvious.

## 3

At the register, an older man froze under the gun's sweep.

"What the fuck are you looking at?" the boy snapped.

"Soccer," the man stammered, voice shaking.

## 4

The coach had meant to leave earlier. But he'd lost his jersey, cursed at traffic, and wound up late again. His ex's text still burned in his pocket: *You missed the photo. The kids are hurt. Maybe this isn't good for them anymore.*

On his way to the fields he'd seen the gold Chrysler sprawled across two spaces. His fist had clenched around his keys.

## 5

Now he stood in the store, facing his former player.

"What happened to you? You were my best defender."

"Life happened. Being Black in the white man's world happened. Parents pulled me out after someone keyed their car. Said soccer was for rich white people."

The boy's voice cracked, then steadied with bitterness.

"Never let me play again."

## 6

The clerk fumbled bills from the register. Shelves gaped half-empty. The air-conditioner banged in the background. On a dusty barrel, someone had traced a sad face in the grime.

"It's not your fault, Coach," the boy said. "You were one of the good ones."

"Give me the gun and go home."

"Can't do that."

"Why not?"

"Because this is what kids like me do. We don't play soccer."

## 7

The last twenty slapped onto the counter. Sirens swelled outside.

"Cops will be here any second," the coach urged. "Go now."

The boy's nostrils flared. *Nowhere to go.*

# 8

Two cruisers skidded to the curb. Doors slammed.

"Leave!" the coach shouted.

Instead, a struggle ignited—older and younger, coach and player, white and black. Arms tangled, the revolver jerking between them. Fluorescents buzzed. The drunk muttered prayers against the cooler.

# 9

In that blur of bodies, two endings flickered:

— A bullet tearing through the boy's skull, his gray matter sprayed against the slushy machine.

— Or the barrel turning, easing the coach's guilt with his own death.

# 10

On a humid night in Fairview, in a sagging corner store where poverty bled into prosperity, a dull Chrysler, a coach, and a boy with a gun found resolution in a single bullet.

# RICHIE LACK

Richie Lack began the year with death. His mother first, his father days later. Grief brushed him, but underneath was something else — a long, low ache that had shadowed him since childhood.

When Richie was six, he clasped his mother's hand.

"Mama, I'll marry you when I grow up."

She laughed. "Oh, that's sweet. But I'm married to Daddy."

From then on, Richie's small face hardened whenever his father entered a room. He snarled and bristled like a cornered animal. The father played along, until the games soured. The mother, for once adored beyond measure, never chose sides.

Richie's affection lengthened into something else — his lips lingering at her neck, his place still in their bed at ten, his eyes following her into the shower, towel ready in his lap. At sixteen, he watched his father press against her at the sink and fled to the basement, Chuck Berry on the radio, his hands frantic over the diagrams in Cosmo and dog-eared Playboys stacked beside childhood trophies.

It was there, under the stairs, that he found the locked box. A dozen Polaroids. His mother, caught and kept. A treasure he returned to, until his father found it and made it vanish. After that, love in the house curdled. Richie left soon after.

He stumbled through adulthood — bankruptcies, nights on the street, women who fled — until he landed managing an adult video store, where he smothered memory with other people's nakedness.

Six months after his parents' deaths, Richie Lack sat in the office of Wilfred Ellis, estate attorney. The lawyer slid a manila envelope across the desk.

"From your father," he said.

The estate was gone to charity. Only an envelope in his father's hand: *She loved you most.*

Richie drove back to the house on Wilford Lane. The basement smelled of mildew and recollection. He pulled the string on the bulb; the faint chink echoed down the stairs. Chuck Berry still hummed in his skull.

He brushed aside old boxes, spread the envelope across his knees, and traced the words of his father.

His palms slick, he peeled it open.

Out spilled the Polaroids. Yellowed, curling at the edges, shadow and flesh blurred by time.

Richie Lack hunched over them in the half-light. His breath hitched. His hand moved.

And once again, he loved his mother most.

# THE THIRD RING

With the vigilance of a prey animal, I watch the IV needle break the skin of my pale arm. The antiseptic smell mixes with sweat, bile creeping up my throat. Beyond the curtain: *blood type, O-negative, double-check.*

The monitor keeps its steady beep. Tubes snake into me. The doctor steps in, says my hemoglobin is low. I could have died.

"My donor card's in there," I tell him, nodding at the bag of belongings on the floor.

"We can discuss that later. Focus on getting better."

"They called me at home," I blurt. He shrugs, leaves.

"They called me!" I shout after him.

The drunk in the next cubicle stirs. "Ya wanna drink my piss?"

I decline.

I try to block out the restraints on my arms and legs, to reorganize the week into clean blocks: dinner 6:15, news 6:30. First Red Cross call Monday, 8:00. First donation Tuesday morning. By Friday, emergency room.

The monitor quickens with my heart. I yell. The drunk joins, banging a bedpan like a cymbal. A pack of nurses rushes in, plunges a giant needle into my thigh. *Psychotic. Haldol.*

As the drug spreads, my thoughts stagger. Nothing in my life happens off schedule. I am not the crazy, paranoid man in the far cubicle. I am efficient. Without attention to detail, life unravels. And now I have a big mess.

It began with a phone call. I answered on the third ring — the perfect number. Not too eager, not too standoffish.

"This is the American Red Cross. Your one donation can save up to three lives…"

I wrote it neatly in my notepad: *Red Cross — Needs Blood.*

Tuesday, again, third ring. Same message. I wrote: *Red Cross — Wants Blood.*

On Wednesday lunch break, I donated. Easy. Painless. I felt useful.

That night, dinner at 6:15, news at 6:30, phone at 8:00, third ring. Same message. I returned to donate again. The woman behind the desk scanned my card. Everything seemed fine.

On my way out I asked how often I could donate. "Eight weeks between whole blood, sixteen for double reds."

I stopped at the door. "But I donated yesterday."

She blinked. Tapped her keyboard. "We have no record of that."

I touched the bandage on my arm. "There must be an error."

Errors are disruptive.

I left. Returned the next day. And the next. And the next. Each time, invisible to the woman at the desk. Until the day I arrived—dizzy, tachycardic, on the verge of collapse. That was not routine.

✛ ✛ ✛

Now, hours after the Haldol, I lie half-floating, calm in a way I have never been. A young psychiatrist sits at the foot of the bed. I prefer people to my right, but I let it go.

He speaks of involuntary commitment, seventy-two hours, court orders. I half-hear. My eyes are on the clock.

"Just wait," I whisper.

At 8:00 p.m., from the bag of belongings labeled with my name, the phone rings. Once. Twice. Three times.

I smile at the perfect number.

"You can answer it," I tell the psychiatrist. "It's the Red Cross."

# SLUM FLOWER

Even daybreak didn't slow the lot lizards. From her Mazda, she watched the sleeper cab of a Peterbilt swallow a scraggy blonde. Six a.m. Turbo Jesus was late. She flicked her cigarette, lit another.

Diesel belched from an eighteen-wheeler, mingling with the fry grease from Big Boy's grill. Around her: the metallic slug of cars at the pumps, the slap of tires over broken asphalt, strangers side-eyeing her in the far corner of the lot.

Her fingers worried the tracks in her arms. Heroin had stripped her body to bone and tendon, left her skin gray, veins knotted, cough ragged. The bend of her right elbow still burned where poison once branched toward her heart.

At a nursing home interview two weeks earlier, she'd hidden the damage under sleeves. Marge from HR didn't look up from her desk. *You start in two weeks.* The halls had reeked of urine, the faces empty as bowls. She left thinking: this is how far I've fallen.

She circled the truck stop like a buzzard over roadkill, then parked in shadow, hoodie swallowing her thin frame. She dozed, waking in time to see another lizard slide from a Peterbilt, half-dressed, heading to scrub herself clean. Not long ago she was that girl, taking veiny flesh into her mouth for a fix. The memory choked her. She cracked the window, let in the air.

It hadn't been childbirth that wrecked her. It was the after: the fights with her husband, the sleepless nights, the isolation. Three months in, she was back on the mother-baby unit, caring for strangers' newborns while she ignored her own. One rough night she stole a Percocet. Then more. Three months later, she met Turbo Jesus and switched to heroin—cheaper, easier, cleaner than robbing the Omnicell.

Turbo drove a battered Civic with *turbo* spray-painted down the quarter panel. The first time, he called her Slum Flower: tall redhead, hair spiraled around her face. He had everything. He was her savior and her undoing. She bit the rotten apple and swallowed hard.

She sold her body. Lost her husband. Abandoned her child. Slept under the Tulip Street Bridge with the others: tents, tarps, burnt spoons, foil scattered on the dirt. Bodies slumped against fences, sprawled across mattresses, hard to tell who was dead.

The Doctor worked behind a bedsheet strung between a cart and a pole. Two dollars for a clean needle. Users nodded for hours, their breath thinning to a hiss.

Once she tried to quit. Three days of agony: hair hurt, nails hurt, every muscle screamed. On the third morning she vomited clotted blood onto the sidewalk. Someone dosed her with Suboxone and dumped her at the ER.

Her family committed her. Rehab. Then NA meetings in a church between a Circle K and a Waffle House. Ex-users hunched in pews, sipping Styrofoam coffee, clutching bibles. By the door sat a basket of clean needles — protection, reminder.

Months clean, a temporary nursing license in hand, she sat in her Mazda waiting for Turbo. She told herself she only wanted half a Perc, a Tramadol. Not to use—just to hold. To prove.

The wind kicked trash across the asphalt. She fingered her long red hair, clean now, combed flat against her neck. She tilted her face to the blue sky and whispered, *Not today.*

Keys in ignition. Then knuckles tapped the glass.

*Slum Flower,* Turbo mouthed with a wink.

And her hands fell.

# PULSE CHECK

Pulling into the lot outside my lover's townhouse, the storm breaks, sending trash down the gutters with the remnants of my confidence. I stall, listening to rain hammer the roof. I dip my hands out the window, rinsing sweat from my face.

The squall slackens. A sparrow jerks a worm from the sod. I need time. The gas station herbs need time. Cheap, Chinese, God-knows-what's-in-them Extenze® pills, bought from a clerk bathed in the blue light of the cigarette display.

In the Circle K lot I asked myself, *What the fuck am I doing?* Decades older, married, trying to be a lover again—sex distilled by marriage, from full-bodied wine to thin two-buck chuck. Her body taut, mine not. After our first time, I asked her what was different with older men.

"It's your skin," she said. "Feels old."

"I am a man," I repeat. The affirmation curdles into a war cry. I've already swallowed more than the package warns, but I empty it anyway. My gut knots, sweat pours in the wrong places, my heart staggers: *dub-lu-dub-lu-lub-dub.*

✛ ✛ ✛

Wipers clack, radio low. I rock in the seat, muttering, "Get hard, motherfucker, get hard." The rectal pressure finally sparks stiffness. A belch rises — bitter, desperate. Time to go in.

Inside, candlelight wavers as Amos Lee croons. I'm dizzy from the three stairs up. Clothes off fast, hers too. I force the urgency, masking the fragility of my body. At the peak of brute exertion—ego, libido, pills, and heart colliding—I plunge into darkness.

I wake tangled in her satin sheets, damp with misfired semen. Fingers trail my chest. I whisper, *I love you,* to soften what I imagine is her disappointment.

There's no answer.

Her hands aren't caressing. She's checking for a pulse.

# PUNISHMENT

With a flick of his fingernail, he decapitates the honeybee, pinching its head and limp proboscis between his fingers. Remorse flickers.

"Punishment?" Mackie Chapman calls, pedaling by on his three-speed.

"No, I…lost something," he mutters.

"Looks like punishment," Mac laughs, popping a wheelie. The cards on his spokes BRRRRAAAP with power.

Alone, he finds a rhythm, shearing high grass with scissors. His father calls it discipline, not punishment. But as the sun burns his neck and the blades blister his hands, he feels only humiliation — neighbors watching him crawl the lawn on his knees.

When his father vanishes from the window, he abandons the scissors and claws at the turf until a hole opens. He crawls inside, knees tight to chest, and screams until the salty brine of the tank water replaces the rancid tang of childhood.

The white-framed house sagged with age: beadboard ceilings, cockeyed windows, floors that creaked like tired bones, darkened where the wood drank too much stain.

A patchwork of smells — candles, sage, oils — clung to the narrow hall. Crystals tickled the glass; a dog dozed in his bed. Beyond was the flotation tank.

His therapist called it a better alternative to alcohol or cannabis. He doubted that, but agreed to try.

After brief instruction from the bandy-legged attendant, he showered and lowered himself in.

Darkness wrapped him, the magnesium brine raising him like a viscous womb. The water matched his body's heat, erasing its borders. Ears submerged, sound vanished. Thoughts pinballed. A tingle on his skin stirred panic. Memory broke loose.

The van door flew open on a back road. He was ten. Everyone screamed but his father, who jerked the wheel and slowed the Ford to the shoulder. His own scream slipped out thin as a whimper. Had he forgotten to lock the door? His mother? Fear poured like lava. He thought of jumping, but his body refused.

At home, rage filled the house. His mother shrank. He hated her for it, though relieved he wasn't the target.

"You idiot!" his father roared. Dishes shattered, doors slammed.

When the fight erupted, he slipped to his room, burying himself under blankets, pounding fists into the mattress until the black universe of the tank consumed him.

At ninety minutes the music came, then the lights. He rinsed, dressed. The thoughts that had surfaced circled the drain and vanished.

"How was your float?" asked the girl at the counter, sitting cross-legged, scraping honey from a frame.

"I think I'll come back," he said, watching the wax cells collapse, the bees already swarming to rebuild.

# THE VISITOR

"What do we do with it?"

"Fuck if I know."

A small crowd gathered in the street, most keeping their distance, some leaning close. With my daughter's hand in mine, I edged forward. Tink Bayman, a bruiser of a man, held its leash—a frayed rope—and led the cloven-hooved creature past us, its stilted march resisting his pull.

Inside the storage building, the crowd pressed into corners. Its tail twitched, nostrils flared, tongue probing the air. The eyes held no fear, only curiosity.

"It's gross," someone said.

"It's an animal," Martha Byrne barked, forcing her way to the front. Few things happened in the village without her.

Then, without warning, the dull-coated beast emptied its bowels on the floor. Martha shrieked. Lee Chin covered her face, others bolted into the moonlight, pale and gagging.

"It can't hurt us," I said. A few nodded.

"How did it get here?" someone asked.

No one knew. There were stories—abandoned abattoirs, rare sightings. But no one alive had seen one.

✛ ✛ ✛

The world had long since collapsed under droughts, floods, and swarms of desperate refugees. Humanity didn't kill the earth—just the things that sustained us. My grandparents spoke of the last swine nursing on its dying mother. After that, the reset began.

✛ ✛ ✛

By nightfall, only a half-dozen remained: Tink, my daughter, Bill Rishovd, Donna Allen, and myself. Curiosity turned to hunger.

"I've read they were delicious," my daughter said. "And fed millions."

"Before India flooded, they were sacred," she added.

Tink tugged the leash. "We might not get another chance."

"To what?" Bill asked.

"To eat it," my daughter snapped. Fourteen going on thirty. "Animals were for eating."

Tink left, returned with an aluminum bat and a crowbar. "She's right. It's a blessing."

No one protested.

✛ ✛ ✛

We circled. My daughter stepped closer, eyes wide. "You sure about this?" I asked.

Tink swung. The animal sidestepped, groaned, but stayed upright. Its eyes widened, still curious.

"Think so," Tink said.

Bill hesitated, crowbar loose. "What do we even do once it's dead?"

Tink snatched it from him, tossed me the bat. "On three. Head."

"One…two…three."

We struck. The creature buckled, blood pooling fast. Tink looped the rope over a beam and hauled. Its neck stretched, hooves clawed for ground.

My daughter moved in. With a shard of glass, she carved one clean line, throat to belly, letting gravity finish the work.

# JUST A BOX

A fogged windshield tested the Volvo's tired defrost. Rain smeared under the wipers as I hunched low, chin on the wheel, squinting into the dark. Avery leaned out the window, shouting her mother's name until the downpour drove her back inside.

"This is ridiculous," I said. "I'm done."

I punched the gas. The Volvo leapt forward.

"Slow down," Avery whispered.

Headlights caught a figure in the street. The bald tires squealed, then the car struck. The belts cinched, the Volvo pitched, and a scream trailed us into a bin of recyclables. Trash scattered over the wet pavement.

I bolted out. Laura Beth lay tangled beneath the wheel, limbs bent monstrous, her pale face buried under blood. I knelt, squeezed her hand, fumbled my phone. As I called 9-1-1, her moan thinned into rain.

Weeks before, every talk had soured into the same fight.

"Trust her," I told Laura Beth. "She's old enough to stay with friends."

"You're lecturing me on trust?" Her hands clutched the hem of her too-large sweater, rising over her abdomen, pausing at the scar across her chest as if to inventory every failure.

"I trusted you'd be there when I needed you most.

"I was," I said.

"Were you?"

She circled the kitchen table, muttering, then burst through the door, circling the house seven times before vanishing into the hedges.

"It's my fault," Avery said. "She hates me." I should've corrected her. I didn't.

When Laura Beth didn't return, we got in the car.

Rain sheeted the street. The Volvo idled on its broken headlight, casting blood across the asphalt.

"Stay in the car!" I shouted, but Avery slipped out, chasing her mother's last breath.

She stumbled at the curb, veered into a yard lit faint by a porch lamp. Then she was gone—disappearing into the darkness, and I feared she'd never return. Her mother's death was too much to witness, too much to absorb.

But she came back, a shadow re-emerging with a box. I caught her kneeling in the grass, cardboard sagging wet in her hands. She tried to press it square around her mother, as if shaping a coffin, but everything gave way.

"It's just a stupid box," she sobbed, kicking at it with her muddy Converse.

Avery had never let things die. When Snowball, our cat, was ripped apart in the engine fan, she locked herself in a closet until I staged a funeral with a mutilated stuffed animal. A proxy death for her to bury.

Laura Beth had raged against it. She dragged Avery downstairs, shoving a scrap of bloody fur into her hand.

"This is Snowball. Dead is dead."

"I hate you," Avery screamed. Nothing was the same after.

Now, soaked through, we dug into the yard until the earth opened wide. Avery and I dragged the heavy inside. I covered it with mud.

"A moment of silence," she said.

We bowed our heads. I cried for her—for the denial I fostered, the wife I broke, the daughter I betrayed. But before I could speak, Avery squeezed my hand.

"It's just a box," she whispered.

# NEST

The first one comes from beneath the refrigerator: antennae probing, underbelly of its exoskeleton scrubbing against the dusty linoleum, its compressed body—near invulnerable to squashing—scuttling into the light.

"Fucking roaches," he yells. Another, then another. He rocks the fridge, crumbs crunching underfoot, insects scattering.

"This is your fault," he says. "You're a slob. Look at this place."

She slips toward the sink, fingernails prying dried food from porcelain as warm water runs across her hands. Behind her, his anger deflates. In the dim kitchen, the dishes clink like bones.

"I'm moving out. You don't appreciate me," she says. "I'm leaving."

Her face uncoils in the mirror. She falls back on the unmade bed. "Who am I kidding?"

As the sun divides the room, a roach scurries over lace panties on the floor, erratic, fearless.

He hunts them with Raid. Flat on his belly, jeans strangling his gut, he drives toxic fog beneath the appliances. He coughs, snot stringing his face, but grins as the roaches writhe into the open, antennae flailing, torsos bucking on their backs until they coil into death.

She can't stop thinking of them. Later, while he snores with his tongue fat and wet against his throat, she wanders the kitchen for ice cream. The house gave a slow shudder. A few survivors skitter across the counter. She touches one, its mahogany shell polished, and lets it crawl across her skin. The prick of its feet makes her shiver.

Soon she's collected a dozen in a Pyrex dish, their bodies bloated and slick, antennae wagging. She listens to their hiss, the scrape of spiny feet. She feels chosen.

Weeks pass. Her prize is the dominant female, swelling as the others breed. She moves it into a twenty-gallon tank warmed by a lamp. She stirs the nest with her hand, letting them climb her wrist, antennae quivering against her flesh. The large female arches and judders, leaving behind a chalk-white smear, her glands open in invitation. Heat rushes through her.

"Your problem is you don't obey me," he chuckles, slapping her ass. He's drunk on extermination, puffed with false manhood. Upstairs he takes her, graceless, insisting on his right. When he's done, he snores.

She rises, straddles his naked body, arms spread like wings. She lowers her mouth to his, releases the roach. It slides down his throat, its chitinous body lodging in his windpipe, wings unfurling. His breath rattles, then stops.

Minutes later, the insect returns. She slips it inside herself, opening in pleasure, making a nest of her own.

# THE FORGETTINGS

Pastor Mike was one of the first. His memory—pink, coiled tight—bounded across the street and vanished into a storm drain. Days later, when a gay couple thanked him for baptizing their baby girl, he denied it ever happened.

"I think he's just a Republican," a parishioner said.

"They always are," another answered.

Donna Bromley's was darker, loose, like a sparrow's nest. It slipped from her head in Starbucks, where a barista swept it into the trash. She forgot her bedridden mother, and for one weekend went to the beach, her first vacation in four years. When she came home, her mother lay dead in a puddle of urine.

"My memory…" she told police. No recollection of the barista, or her mother.

A boy jumped into his family pool and drowned. He had forgotten his terror of water. His sister had forgotten she was supposed to be watching him. His lost memory glistened at the bottom of the pool, while hers quivered beneath her bed, red and purple with guilt.

Elsewhere, a wife of twenty-five years forgot she was married and shot her husband as he came in from the yard. A doctor in Michigan told a man he had terminal cancer; by the time he left the hospital chapel, he had forgotten—his lost memory a metastatic mass without power. He surprised his wife with a vacation instead.

A Klansman missed his meeting when he forgot which way to turn at the crossroads. His memory rolled into a swamp and was eaten by an alligator. He picked up a dark-skinned man, attended a bayou reunion, and married the man's cousin a year later.

Scientists called it unintentional cognitive offloading—the mind saturated, memories scattered everywhere. Experts spoke of dendrites and hippocampi until they forgot what they were there to explain.

The president was scheduled to calm the nation. At the podium he lost his way. Instead he asked the chaplain of Seal Team 5 to pray for our men in Iraq—exposing a classified deployment.

His memory, flag-colored—red, white, blue—tumbled from his shoulders and broke. Colors bled across his shoes.

And the cameras kept rolling.

# CATCH AND RELEASE

They stomped a patch of plume grass flat by the pond, set down their poles and tackle, and opened the folding chair whose canvas belly held their lunch. Clouds pushed the blue aside.

Grandfather's spot lay at the end of a rasping gravel road beside an abandoned farm: a tractor rusting into wildflowers, a thresher swallowed by weeds, a sagging *No Trespassing* sign.

"Storm's moving in," he said, squinting at the horizon.

Darla dug through the tackle box until she found the lure she wanted, tucked a streak of purple hair under her cap, and fitted the jig onto her line.

"This is where I met your grandmother," he said, toes edging the water, searching for his reflection.

Since she was old enough, they'd fished here. He always claimed his generation was the last good lot, this pond the last place worth casting. Darla mouthed the words with him.

"Other ponds are stocked with trash."

She wanted to roll her eyes but bit her lip instead.

"Half an hour before weather hits," he said—his way of shifting from fights to forecast.

"Just want something special," she said, casting toward the shadowed corner.

Her lure plopped among the waxy lilies. A ripple followed, then another followed: lean, purple, gleaming.

"Over there," she said.

"A nibble."

He squinted, sea-captain serious. Before she could pull, the line went taut.

"Got something."

"I hope it's not one of those trans things," he muttered. "Toss it back if it is."

"In my day, two options. Man or woman. None of this fashionable nonsense."

"My gender's fluid," she said.

He rummaged the tackle box. Lures rattled like loose teeth.

"Do you love me less?" she asked, pulling hard, rod bent near double.

"No..." he said.

✛ ✛ ✛

The minutes dragged, cold and silent, each one a small tax on her choices—the cost of acceptance.

Then the water heaved: the pale belly broke the surface, thrashed, vanished.

Darla dug her heels into the mud and reeled until the fish slapped onto the bank, gasping.

Grandfather rose, caught the line in his fist, studied the body.

"White male," he said. "Wrong kind."

He flung it back. The splash spread, then smoothed flat.

"No harm in catch and release. Maybe you'll get lucky, like I did."

Darla watched the pond swallow everything, and whispered:

"I hope so."

# BENEATH THE CRAPE MYRTLE

He collapsed as if a thief had looted his bones. The poison was swift, merciful. For a moment it might have looked like fainting, but the twisted arm, the crooked leg, the mop of hair veiling his eyes told the truth.

I held his hand. Used my sleeve to shutter the tears. Stayed until the dark overtook the light. His death was quick, and for that I was grateful. I had promises to keep—sealed in hugs, bound in a wife's deathbed plea.

Just days ago I became less father than killer. I'd bartered for the vial at the boundary where the classes divide. We had agreed: suffering was worse than death. As his body stilled, I whispered *forgive me* and vomited beside him.

For eleven years Samuel was all brightness—curious, gentle, human. His mother died giving him life, a hemorrhage she could not survive. Her last words: *Please… let him be human.*

We were one of the few who refused modification. Others re-engineered their children for perfect health. We kept the DNA pure. It cost me everything.

One night Samuel stumbled in, toothbrush in hand, paste and blood pooling in his mouth. *Daddy, why am I bleeding?*

The diagnosis came fast: acute lymphocytic leukemia. Within weeks bruises flowered, his bones filling with rot. At night he wept in his sleep. Awake, he pleaded: *Don't let me suffer.*

Clinics turned us away. The official protocol was termination, the polite word for disposal of unmodifieds. I heard my wife's voice again: *Let him be human.* So I did.

On a warm fall day I dug the hole beneath the crape myrtle and placed him beside his mother. Superman toy for him. A gold chain for her. Traditional burial was forbidden. I did it anyway.

Years passed. I spent hours beneath that tree, until the years turned me stale. Rage grew with forgetting. One day I noticed the chair beneath the crape myrtle and couldn't recall why it stood there. Another time, I found Superman in the grass, a chain caught on the chair's leg. Both had risen through the soil. Curious artifacts, I thought, pocketing them. Did they belong to me? Had I lived here long? Did I once have a family?

Memory came and went like weather. Debris of a shipwreck's treasure—bright for a moment, then gone.

I grew too old for effort, too old for purpose. I cried out—for Samuel, for the mother and wife, for the unmodified, for the cost of being human. Termination would be my path in the morning, as it was Samuel's—not from disease, but from living a full life, and forgetting.

That night I lay in bed, Superman and the necklace on the nightstand. I stared until their memory slipped away. Then sleep took me.

# THE MESSIAH

*"For I am under authority myself and have soldiers under me, and I say to one man, but the children of the kingdom will be thrown out into the darkness."– Matthew*

"Friend or enemy?" the stranger asked, rifle leveled at my face.

Too tired to be afraid, I nudged the barrel away.

"Just a man," I said. "Headed south."

He lowered the gun and offered his hand. "You're welcome to join our pilgrimage."

That was three days ago.

"Where's Zechariah?" I asked.

The Messiah lengthened his stride, metal bottles clanking on the pack at his back. Behind us trailed the procession—refugees hidden beneath turbans, masks, visors, rags. Sunburnt, coughing, bent by hunger.

When the grid collapsed, everyone fled somewhere. I fled south. What followed was a blur of heat and pain. At times, I pictured the hand of God, focusing sunlight through a magnifying glass, burning us like the ants I torched as a boy.

The Messiah's beard spilled to his chest, his hair matted to his shoulders, his eyes hollow. He quoted scripture like a jukebox. Zechariah had named him the Messiah.

Zec was a widowed engineer from Virginia, a fisherman with a limp and a smile. He wasn't driven by fear—just boredom.

"I won't be around much longer," he told me once. "Others like me haven't fared well."

The Messiah picked at him daily, verse after verse, until one morning Zec was gone.

"Zechariah went it alone," the Messiah said. "On a different path."

I knew it was a lie.

"Fallen! Fallen is Babylon the Great!" – Revelation 18:2

"You'll take his place," the Messiah said.

"My turn to be tested?"

"The world is different now. We must repent."

I'd never been religious. But after the collapse, everyone prayed. Except Zec.

Outside Wilsonville I pressed back. "Where's your family?"

"Dead." His tone hollow.

"Zec didn't leave, did he?"

His eyes measured me. "For evildoers and non-believers will be cut off, but those who wait for the LORD will inherit the land."

I said nothing.

"If we confess our sins, he is faithful…" – 1 John 1:9

✢ ✢ ✢

By Georgia, heat had stripped me raw. My shirt in tatters, my body a map of bites and sores. The Messiah handed me a pill bottle.

It was my wife's Oxycodone.

"You stole this," I said.

He nodded, his hand tight on the rifle.

"When my wife was dying, I took her pills," I said. "I thought it would ease my pain." She knew. "It destroyed us."

The Messiah bucked. "Nor thieves, nor the greedy will inherit the kingdom of God."

"I was just trying to survive her cancer."

He stiffened. "Do you consider yourself worthy of redemption?"

"I made mistakes. But everyone deserves a second chance."

He raised his rifle, finger brushing the trigger. "As I am the Messiah, I am he. And I judge you not worthy."

# THE LEDGER OF SMALL WARS

I tried to be him. I failed. So I took to the bottle. Could've chosen vein, pipe, or pills. I gag on pills and fear needles. My hang-ups chose my path.

Most mornings, whiskey pours before I clear my head. The kick buys a minute of mercy, and then the burden returns—like a census worker with a clipboard, knocking.

✛ ✛ ✛

The motel hums—bees in the drywall, old air in the vent talking to itself.

I emptied my pockets into the drawer: candy wrappers folded small as origami, an old newspaper clipping brittle as dried leaves, a chipped Superman no taller than my thumb. Proof of a life carried piece by piece, never spent, never thrown away. An envelope of photographs that burns the hand that holds it.

Here's the ledger I can't keep straight:

I was the Irish Twin on the porch, blackberry thorns in my calves, a tall boy whispering penny candy from the briers. I was the brother who went up the hill for a favor and came down smaller.

I learned the chair first—father planted, radiator knocking its gospel: just trapped air. We never found the valve for love.

I was the paper boy under an iron sky, snow like static, drafted into the Winter War by a voice only I could hear. The route became trenches. The bundle hit the dumpster and thumped like a body.

I was the boy who lived on Grandmother's Pop-Tarts and soap operas, who loosened the basement valve and watched my parents curse in cold water while the old woman smiled into the end of the world: Luke and Laura again.

I was the snow-globe man's child—my father sealed in his translucent ark, palm to plastic at my wedding, stormlight pinwheeling across his face.

"The worst hasn't come," he shouted. "I will never leave."

I was the Patriot in tights, a box-made boy with a wooden repeater, the schoolyard tuned to wolf. I learned what a costume can't protect.

I was the crow's witness, my sister swearing they were memory keepers and would lift her out. They did. Straight to the graveyard.

I was the fake superhero with the red mask who bled through it anyway, and the man years later who opened a trapdoor in a snowbank and found the old tracksuit sagging like a saint's robe. I put it on and went where the bully slept.

I stood at the foot of a rehab bed, the boy's heart steady. After snorting poison off porcelain, I learned a new species of prayer.

At thirteen I was the naked boy with the crossbow bolt in the headboard, sprinting bare across wet grass while the toddle sang *Daddy* and the town turned to look.

I was the man who said I am a winner, and believed it long enough to empty a van of misfits into the night—Linda in the pig hauler, Tina in the creek, Charlie, white foam still. The ticket never paid.

I lay on a hill with Dandelion, my palm on her flat belly, wishing for absence and calling it mercy. Seeds let go and I envied them.

I sat in a coastal clinic with Lillian under a chandelier heavy enough to crush us.

"Blue eyes or no cancer," the man said.

Compromise is a kind of slow violence. Love, a refusal to look away.

I stood between dish and sky, the signal washing through my skull: recipes, rehab shows, porn—the world piped into me. My wife kissed my forehead and set me in the yard like a busted appliance. Then her voice came on the carrier wave, thinner and truer than the woman herself. The signal never ends.

The box came with our name in gold. Cake in HR. A daughter who said, *don't make me ashamed.* At zero the lid sighed and the dark inside had teeth. The box did what boxes do: kept. We did what we always do: step in.

I answered the payphone on the third ring—the perfect number—and the line was dead. Or I was.

I brought a Dirt Devil to clean a lifetime of sin. I strangled it with my own hands. Plastic casing split. My wrist opened. Blood sprayed FREE across the asphalt—a mantra I couldn't live up to. Fine print is a razor blade.

I scrolled Phantom Beach until sand lived in my pockets and my girlfriend smashed the screen. The salt stayed. Desire is the talent for summoning bodies that aren't there.

I stepped into the recovery pod with my iPhone welded to my palm and came out short a hand. Fine print again.

I worked shift work—Willie whispering cleaning day, Patsy's arms breaking my nose, Catherine unbuckling what I couldn't name. We called it routine. It was communion.

I rang a bell in Wilmington and took Elizabeth's twenty-two frames. Bruises in every finish. I carried them back and a stranger said Elizabeth had been dead for years. A fresh bruise kneaded under the stranger's sleeve. I don't need them, she said, which is another way of saying I can't survive them.

In Fairview I passed a gold Chrysler.

"You were my best defender," the coach said to the boy with the gun. Two endings flickered; one bullet chose.

I was Richie Lack under the stairs, Polaroids like relics, loving the mother most because there was no other way to love.

I donated on Monday, again on Tuesday, again on Wednesday, and by Friday I was strapped to a hospital bed, bound to the language of the third ring, waiting for the Red Cross to call the perfect number so the psychiatrists could hear it.

I met Slum Flower in a parking lot at dawn. Turbo Jesus winked; her hands fell. Under the bridge, mercy sold behind a bedsheet. Sobriety, a riverbed cracked to map-lines.

I took pills in a Circle K lot, told myself I was a man, and woke in satin sheets while a young woman checked my pulse like a thief at the till.

I lay still in a tank where magnesium brine erased the border of my skin and I became only breath and a memory I couldn't bend into something kinder.

I hit Laura Beth with the Volvo in rain thick as secrets, and my girl knelt in the yard trying to square a soaked cardboard coffin. It's just a box, she said. It wasn't, and was.

I learned to love nest roaches for their honesty. They skittered without disguise, their movement a confession. They carried their hunger naked. They left their need undressed by language. They survived, and in that survival there was a kind of truth.

Then came the Forgettings. A president's red-white-blue memory burst onstage and the cameras didn't blink. A barista swept. A daughter found a weekend of sun. A boy forgot the deep; a sister forgot to watch; the pool kept what it keeps. A Klansman missed his turn and married at the crossroads of race and history. Sometimes forgetting saves better than faith.

We fished the old pond—catch and release. My grandfather said other waters were stocked with trash. I pulled up a white belly. He called it the wrong kind, flung it back, and the pond erased him.

I dug under the crape myrtle and put my boy down beside the woman who asked me to keep him human. Years later, Superman and a gold chain rose from the dirt, as if the earth forced remembrance. On bad days I clutched them both and pretended they belonged to someone else.

The Messiah walked south. He said Zechariah took another path; I believed him until I didn't. He lifted my wife's Oxy and called it judgment. I confessed to survive the moment and he leveled the rifle like the old covenant.

The motel AC wheezes. Bees keep talking in the wall.

I pour two fingers and hold off. I stare at the envelope of photographs on the bedspread. In the mirror—sallow, warped—I'm a man-shaped smear.

One voice says all this is borrowed. Another pours a drink and tells me to get on with it.

The crow tilts its head on the sill, takes dictation.

I break the seal.

# ACKNOWLEDGMENTS

I want to thank Unsolicited Press—at the time an all-female press—for taking a chance on the work of a man. Their faith shoved me forward, convinced me maybe my words carried some weight. Without that acceptance I might've walked away, never bothered again. Since then I've written mostly nonfiction—hundreds of thousands of words, the kind that paid the bills, kept the lights on. For that, I owe everything to a small, stubborn press out of Portland, Oregon.

No bullshit. Just books.